Not Guilty

Robert S. Baker

Not Guilty

Robert S Baker

Paperback Edition First Published in the United Kingdom
in 2016 by aSys Publishing

eBook Edition First Published in the United Kingdom
in 2016 by aSys Publishing

Copyright © Robert S Baker

Robert S Baker has asserted his rights under 'the Copyright
Designs and Patents Act 1988' to be identified as
the author of this work.

All rights reserved.

No part of this book may be reproduced or transmitted in any
form or by any means, electronic, mechanical, photocopying,
recording, or otherwise, without prior written
permission of the Author.

Disclaimer

This is a work of fiction. Names, characters, businesses, places, events
and incidents are either the products of the author's imagination or
used in a fictitious manner. Any resemblance to actual persons, living or
dead, or actual events is purely coincidental.

ISBN: 978-1535096911

aSys Publishing
http://www.asys-publishing.co.uk

Chapter 1

Deception

James, a gifted student with straight A's in all subjects, quiet and reserved, preferred to keep to himself during school; he was not interested in the girls and didn't socialise. He preferred to work on his computer studying, trying to achieve a good future for himself, but running the gauntlet every morning of jealous pupils not having the intelligence to match his grades and who enjoyed making fun of him.

He was tall with short black hair, with good features. He prided himself on staying tidy and smart and always felt he should be presentable. Many of the other students hated him for his accomplishments, none more so than Jennifer Collins. She would have to take her exams again to achieve better grades. She'd taken James aside, asking him to help, pressing her chest against him. He pulled away: "I'll help you study but that's it," he said firmly

She wanted him to hack into the school computer to acquire the answers for her exam paper. He refused, which was something she was not used to hearing, considering she was one of the prettiest girls in the school and most of the boys would do anything for her.

She paraded herself, flaunting and teasing the boys at every opportunity she had. She was a natural blonde, not like most of the girls at school who were peroxide. She had a good figure of ample proportions. She would hang around with others girls who weren't quite so pretty. She had been known to take drugs, and even smoke cannabis behind the garages when she was not in school. Jennifer conjured a plan to get her own back on James because he wouldn't help her.

James walked home on his own as he always did through the narrow alleyways. Jennifer and her friends came up from behind him and called out his name. He turned round to see who had called him. Jennifer threw a pair of her knickers which he grabbed to stop them from hitting his face. He threw them back to her. She smiled, "Thanks, you're not prepared to help me then, James?"

"I told you Jennifer, no I'm not hacking into the school computers," he said firmly, continuing to walk.

Jennifer and her friends following took another alleyway into a derelict building. Jennifer ripped her knickers James had thrown back to her. She knew his DNA would be on her knickers, she changed into the ripped knickers. Her friends dragged her blazer in the dust. Jennifer ripped her blouse making sure it was obvious she'd been attacked. Her friends left, Simone and Jackie went home.

Jennifer phoned the police on her mobile sobbing. The police came immediately listened to her invented story as she trying to cover her breast with her ripped blouse, how James had attacked her and dragged into the old building on the way home from school. She said she was only trying to be friends with him, he wanted more and she wasn't interested. Then he started to force her and after she screamed he ran off.

Her clothes were taken for DNA testing and James's DNA was found on the knickers. James was arrested immediately, expelled from school and ended up in a detention centre after the courts ruled he should spend three months there for the unprovoked attack. During the three months of his detention. His parents had disowned him and told him never to come home again.

He'd been attacked himself by two inmates and received several beatings. Rape is something that is not tolerated in prison by other inmates. His parents had sent most of his personal effects, including the small amount of savings he had to the prison for him to collect on his release.

James was devastated, he'd done absolutely nothing wrong and to make matters worse, no one would believe him. His career prospects were over and his education was finished as far as he was concerned. One or two of the inmates who did speak to him, told him to get his own back. The more he sat and thought over the events leading him to his present situation and dwelling on the subject for some time, he started to become angry.

Not Guilty

The only clothes he possessed were his school uniform. Once he'd been released he ripped the badge off the pocket and threw it on the floor. There was no one there to meet him as he left the prison. He was on his own and that's the way he liked it.

Chapter 2

Starting Over

He hadn't been registered as a sex offender through some mix-up. He collected his few belongings from the prison and made his way into London, living rough for a while. He grew a beard and let his hair grow long, so no one would recognise him. He had a stroke of luck after changing his name. He acquired employment working with computers at a mail order company. He found some digs and after a few months, life was starting to turn around. He saved enough money to buy himself a laptop; finding Jennifer's webpage, he started chatting online with her and she didn't realise it was him; this went on for a few weeks.

He told her he was very wealthy and lived in London, which was a hundred miles away from where she lived. He was determined to have his own back one way or another. Within a month, he had passed his driving test; another expense he could ill afford but it was essential if it wanted to be mobile. He purchased an old white courier van with nearly 300,000 miles on the clock, which cost him a great deal to insure because of his age.

He was now just over 18, but felt very proud of himself considering what he'd just suffered. James took two weeks holiday from his employment and drove to a place called Long Marston. There used to be an old army base there. He wandered around the derelict buildings searching for somewhere he could hide a captive. He removed some rubble covering an old steel trap door, finally prying it free.

He shone his torch down the ladder and proceeded to descend. Once he'd reached the bottom it opened up into an old bunker. He tried the light switch and much to his surprise, the lights came on. It was quite damp down there, but could be made habitable with a bit of work. He spent three days cleaning the place up; there were even three old beds.

He kept in contact with Jennifer, telling her he would soon come to see her. He was purchasing property in the area. She was extremely excited thinking she was meeting a very wealthy young man, especially as he could supply her with drugs and the good life. He had finished all the modifications he needed to do to make the bunker habitable again.

He phoned Jennifer. "I'm coming down tomorrow night, where would you like to meet?"

She suggested she bring two other friends and meet at the back of the Pheasant pub on the outskirts of the village. James advised her he would meet her there at 8:30 PM. He parked the old van little way down the road and walked the short distance to the back of the pub.

Jennifer looked him up and down along with her two friends. He was wearing a very smart suit, his beard and shoulder length hair disguised him sufficiently, she didn't recognise him.

They shook hands. "Where is the stuff" Jennifer enquired eagerly.

"I'm not that stupid. This could have been a trap. It's back in my storage place. You can either come and look at it there or forget it the deal is off," he said firmly.

The three girls looked at each other. Jackie said: "I don't like the sound of that, we don't know him from Adam."

Jennifer asked, "How much stuff have you got with you?"

"More than you've money to pay for, about half a mil," James voiced calmly.

"You mean half a million?" Jennifer smiled.

The £'s were rolling in her eyes, she'd only been able to supply small amounts of drugs to her old school friends in the past because she could never get enough at the right price.

"Yes, half million is nothing I'm off to Birmingham tonight. I have an order for £250,000 worth of crack. I suppose I better go, you lot haven't the money and you're only small time."

James started to walk away. Jennifer grabbed his arm.

"You're right I'm only small time, but I want to be big-time. I want to make money will you help me? You supply me and I'll supply the kids."

"Oh, I don't know if I can be bothered with you."

"Please Johnny," she pleaded.

That was the name he'd pick for myself to use for the deception. Jackie and Simone followed nervously. Jennifer was gripping his arm tightly. She wasn't going to miss any opportunity to become rich.

"You realise you'll have to be blindfolded. I'm not going to let you see where I stash round here. I don't care who you are."

"That's okay, I understand," Jennifer said quickly turning round to the other girls following, "Come on you two stop dragging your feet. We could finally be making lots of money."

Jackie and Simone jumped in the back of the van and James shut the back doors. He'd removed the handle from the inside of the doors so they couldn't be opened internally. Jennifer jumped into the front with James without hesitation. Her smile was broad; all she could think off was the money.

"Put the sunglasses on so you can't see."

Jennifer did everything without question. This was going far better than James had thought. He had a large knife down the side of his door, just in case things went really wrong. He drove them to the Long Marston army camp, parking the old van in a disused shed.

Jennifer went to remove her glasses and he stopped her. "Not yet, wait until I come round your side." He removed some plastic ties from inside his door panel and went round to Jennifer's door. She stepped and out from his coat pocket he removed rolls of tape and quickly covered her mouth. She started to struggle. He then tied her hands behind her back with the cable. The other girls were shouting.

"What's going on?" He placed a cable tie around Jennifer's ankles to stop her kicking and fighting. She was lying on the ground powerless. James removed an imitation gun from behind the seat. He went to the back door and opened it pointing the gun at the two girls. "You even breathe and I'll blow you away, you get the message?" They both nodded, trembling, "One at a time out of the van," he instructed; they did exactly as they were told. He gagged and tied them both the same as Jennifer.

Using a rope, he lowered them down to the bottom of the bunker one at a time, which was a struggle. He removed all their mobiles so they couldn't send a message to anyone, and stamped on them and removed the batteries. He threw each girl on one the beds they looked horrified. Finally, he was going to get his own back for being sent to prison for something he didn't do.

Chapter 3

Payback

He ripped the tape from Jennifer's mouth, holding the knife to her throat. She didn't utter a word. "Do you know who I am, Jennifer?" She moved her head from side to side slowly. "Do you remember the lies you told about me?" Jennifer's eyes enlarged; she knew who it was.

She muttered "I'm sorry, I'm sorry, I shouldn't have done that, please don't kill me. I won't say anything, take us home."

"Yeah, I bet you'd love to send me back to prison, wouldn't you fucking bitch and the other two, you're as bad as her."

They shook their heads from side to side violently. "You can scream all you like but no one will hear you down here," James smiled.

James looked at Jennifer as he sat on the side of her bed. "Let me show you Jennifer what I'm going to do to you. I'll give you a free demonstration."

"Please don't hurt anyone James we are really sorry for what we did to you. Please just let us go. We won't say a word to anyone. We all promise, don't we girls."

Simone and Jackie nodded in desperation. James moved easing Simone from her bed. She hopped across to the wall in front of Jennifer's bed. He cut the ties on her hands and stuck the knife immediately in her throat, she didn't flinch. He slid her hands into a noose hanging from the roof. He pulled on the rope until her hands were stretched above her head and the rope was tight. Jennifer started to scream James moved over and replaced the tape on her mouth.

"That'll shut you up bitch now watch closely," he smiled, walking to a cupboard and removing a notepad and pen. James walked over and sat beside Jackie. She stared at him in horror, fearing for her life. "Would you like to live Jackie"? She nodded quickly, trying to talk through the tape. "Will you be quiet if I remove your tape?" She nodded quickly.

James removed the tape from her mouth and placed the knife to her throat. He then cut the ties from her hands. She rubbed her wrists as they were starting to go numb. "I want you to write exactly what happened the day you three set me up on a rape charge. If you do I'll probably let you go, if you don't, need I say more."

She didn't hesitate. She started writing the tears ran down her cheeks. "Don't wet the paper Jackie, this must be your confession and yours alone." She nodded. She did exactly as she was asked and in two pages wrote a detailed document.

James read it after she'd finished revealing the plan, why Jennifer had instructed her to help, and Simone had even signed. "Please let me go now James, I've done as you asked." James gently placed the tape over her mouth again. She looked horrified as he cable-tied her wrists to the steel bed frame. He then walked over to Simone. "You want to die, Simone?" he asked calmly. She shook her head from side to side, crying.

He removed the tape from her mouth. "Would you like to write a confession?"

"Yes anything I don't want to die," she pleaded. "It was Jennifer that made us help, it was nothing to do with Jackie and me."

Jennifer stared horrified, knowing that the two statements would condemn her. James released the rope holding Simone's arms in the air, and helped her back to her bed to sit down. He passed her the notepad, saying. "Don't forget to include that she sells drugs to the kids at the school." Simone nodded, "Okay," she said quietly. She sat there writing a detailed document listing her part in the attempted rape charge. He then replaced the tape on her mouth and secured her to the bed the same as Jackie.

James moved back to Jennifer's bed, removing the tape from her mouth. She shouted, "You silly bitches, you've condemned us all. He wouldn't kill us."

James replaced the tape. She shook her head in protest. He eased her to her feet and strung her up with the rope so her arms were above her head. She was a hard bitch and didn't give a sod about anybody else except herself.

He searched her denim jacket pocket and found £1000, which he confiscated. She wouldn't need that where she was going. He walked back and sat on Jackie's bed. "Do you want to live? What will you do to persuade me?" he said.

James removed the tape from her mouth. "I will do absolutely anything. I will really," she panicked. He moved to Simone's bed. "What will you do? Do you want to live?" he asked, removing the tape. "Anything you ask me I really will do, I don't want to die please."

He placed his finger to his lips. "Be quiet both of you, the first one that doesn't do as she's told will die, you understand me, you too." They both nodded eagerly. He released Jackie apart from where she was strapped around the ankles so she couldn't run. She smiled with relief. He did the same to Simone.

They hopped until they were side-by-side. "Jackie, do you really like Jennifer or you just do as you're told by her?"

"We both do as we are told she's very nasty when she doesn't get her own way and she gets other girls to pick on us."

"So you suffered like me, only I went to prison and you just got picked on." They nodded. "Well it's payback time girls for her or all of you if you disobey me. I will guarantee you will walk out of here alive, providing you do as I say."

They both smiled. "Thank you." They said together.

"First of all go and wash your face in the basin over there. Both of you I don't want to see make up running down your face. And while you're about it, wash hers."

They did exactly as James requested. Jennifer was shaking her head in protest and trying to break free from the ropes, kicking out with her legs. James tied her ankles to the pipework so she couldn't kick any more.

He set up a video camera fixed on Jennifer. "Jackie move closer to Jennifer now kiss her on the lips, just so I can see I have the camera set right." She did exactly as he requested without question. He then realised he'd left the tape on her lips. He went over and removed the tape "Do it again Jackie." He started filming again. "That's better and don't move till I tell you to move either of you." They did exactly as he said he removed a Stanley knife from his pocket.

"You can go first Simone." Simone looked horrified. "I suggest you stop shouting Jennifer and don't move otherwise you could end up getting hurt." She stopped immediately and stared at the camera. "Jackie put the tape back over her mouth. Simone cut her denim jacket off." Jennifer stared on in horror daring not to flinch as Simone carried out his instructions James stopped the camera. "Right, come back to me and give the Stanley knife to Jackie. Jackie cut the buttons off her blouse, and move to the side, so we can see everything." She did as she was requested and he stopped the camera again, "Now open her blouse and cut her bra between her breasts and cut her blouse away altogether."

Jackie didn't hesitate. Jennifer was now topless James stopped the camera. "Well done girls, now Simone unbutton her denim jeans and pull them right down, including her pants." He started the camera rolling again. She did exactly as he requested. He now had shots of Simone and Jackie removing Jennifer's clothes. He removed the tape from Jennifer's mouth. She sobbed, "If you want to fuck me get on and do it, stop torturing me, it won't be the first man I've slept with to get what I want"

"I've never been with a woman."

"Oh you're fucking gay."

"No I'm not I've never had the opportunity. I was too busy studying until you messed my life up," he shouted.

She scoffed, "Let me free and I'll give you a ride you've never had."

"No thanks. I don't know where you've been," she spat at him.

He walked away back to the camera. Jackie and Simone sat on the bed. Jennifer shouted: "Have a threesome video."

"Now I want you three kissing and cuddling a video to watch later," he laughed.

Jennifer smiled, "That's okay with me. Simone and Jackie get over here." They didn't move; they looked to James for instructions. Jackie passed the Stanley knife back to him. "Go on then girls do as she says," he said. They hopped back over to Jennifer and she removed her clothes, sliding her jeans down to her ankles because the ankles were still tied. He videoed them, kissing and cuddling. This was more than he'd hoped for; his plan was falling into place. "Okay, I've seen enough, dress, you two."

"Come on then, let me go, I've done what you've asked, or do you still wanna fuck me. I forgot you don't know how," Jennifer laughed.

James was surprised at her boldness considering the position she was in. She was feeling confident she was going to be released. He replaced the tape on her mouth, which rather took her by surprise. "What do you think we ought to do to her next, Jackie?" Jackie shrugged her shoulders.

"I just want to go home. I don't care what happens to her." He fetched two syringes from the cupboard. They were already primed full of drugs enough to kill an elephant. He gave one syringe to each girl. "Just inject her in the arm both of you." They stared, alarmed.

"What is it?" Simone asked, trembling.

"Just something to knock her out."

"Why two syringes?" Jackie asked.

"Because it's a very mild sedative and you can't get enough in one syringe."

They reluctantly went over to Jennifer. James videoed as they injected her; within a few minutes she lost consciousness. He took the syringes from the two girls: "You two have finally killed her."

They stared at each other and then at James. "Really, we killed her?" They both burst into tears. "We'll be prosecuted for murder, oh God what are we going to do?" Simone said, panicking.

"Don't panic, calm yourselves. This is what you will do. I'll take you home. You tell the police when they question you that you left her at the pub and she went off with a man in the car. That's the last you saw of her."

James released Jennifer's body from the rope and wrapped her in a plastic sheet. He slung her over his shoulder and climbed the ladder, throwing the body in the back of his van. He then returned sitting on the bed by Simone and Jackie, who was starting to shiver. He placed his arm around their shoulders and they cuddled him. They sat there for a little while and then he collected his film equipment and took it up to the van, returning again.

He knocked the tap of the water pipe in the corner. "Come on girls, let's get out of here." He suddenly remembered he'd left their statements in the cupboard, so he quickly grabbed them before leaving the bunker.

The girls climbed into the front of the van. "Please wear the spectacles so you don't know where we are." They did without question and he drove a little way into the country, where he found a deep ditch. He removed Jennifer's body and rolled it into the ditch where it was covered by undergrowth. He continued, driving back towards the village.

He remarked. "You've got your stories straight girls, don't try and pull a fast one because you're lost this time." They both agreed. He let them out of the van just before the pub and drove off, selecting a route home to London that didn't involve motorways where his van could be picked up on the cameras that would give a time and date of his whereabouts.

He finally arrived home and hid his camera equipment under the floorboards, then replaced the wardrobe on top. He had a few days holiday remaining, so he took his old van to the scrapyard and watched it crushed, so now there was no chance of finding any evidence from the van.

He hoped they wouldn't find her body too quickly or the girls might blab. He watched the news day after day and heard nothing of any interest. He used the £1000 he'd taken from Jennifer to buy himself a small second-hand car. The only news on the telly was of a girl going missing, with a picture of Jennifer. The girls had obviously stuck to the story. He returned to work after a couple more days had passed.

The police interviewed him, checking his small dilapidated flat but found no evidence to link him to the crime. They did ask where the van had gone after they checked DVLA for his vehicle records, but then concluded the van had been destroyed the day before she went missing as far as they were concerned.

Her body was not found for a further six months and by that time nature had taken its course and her body had started to decompose and was virtually unrecognisable. James was very proud of his accomplishment.

Chapter 4
A New Job

James had acquired new employment fitting security alarms to private properties around the country, which meant an awful lot of travelling. A van was provided after six weeks training and his ability to learn quickly meant he was soon on his way to success.

He was sent to Ross on Wye to fit a new alarm. On his arrival, the house was massive and he'd probably have to stay overnight to finish the work. He booked a room at the local pub.

He pulled into the driveway after being let in through the electric gates. The owner met him as he was leaving in his Rolls-Royce. "Good morning, sir, I'm here to install your alarms," James said politely.

"Good morning young man, Mrs Johnson is in the house, she'll see to everything you need, and plug her into the mains while you're at it please," He smiled, "Are you married, son?"

"No sir." James was rather taken back by the question.

"Good chap stay single and sensible," the bald headed chap said, driving away.

James rang the doorbell. A leggy blonde came to the door in a see-through dressing gown. "Oh, you've come to fit the alarms?"

"Yes madam."

"This way." James followed her to the back of the house where there was a heated swimming pool in the back garden. "Alarm everything, I don't want to be disturbed or broken into."

James went back to the van, phoned his boss and told him it would be a two-day job, the place was massive. His boss told him not to worry, they could afford it.

James took his ladders round the back and started fitting sensors and emergency lighting. The property was owned by the Johnsons, they were multimillionaires and he worked in London.

Mrs Johnson was in the swimming pool with not a stitch of clothing on, lying on her back on purpose so that her breasts could be seen through the top of the water along with the rest of her.

James concluded she was nothing but a tart or a money grubber, she couldn't have been a day over 26 and to be with an old goat like her husband it was pretty obvious she was just enjoying the high life.

She continually smiled at James as he worked away knowing full well she was showing him everything. By nightfall James had completed half the work he could hear Mrs Johnson on the telephone.

"So you're stopping in bloody London again tonight." She slammed the phone down and stormed off into the kitchen. James packed his tools away ready to go to the pub, where he'd booked a room for the night. He'd just settled in, had an evening meal and a couple of glasses of wine and was about to retire to bed.

He received a phone call from Mrs Johnson. Apparently he'd left something on the stairway and she'd slipped on it. He drove immediately back to the property. She opened the front door limping on one leg. "I do apologise madam; I didn't think I'd left anything behind."

He then suddenly realised she was limping on the other leg. "Come with me," she insisted. She led him into the lounge and invited him to sit on the settee. She placed her leg on his lap and then threw him a jar of cream.

"Rub some on my ankle gently. It hurt so much after falling on your tool. In fact, put some on both ankles. They both hurt."

James obliged, gently applying the cream not wishing to be sacked by his boss, although he knew he wasn't negligent and he definitely didn't leave any tools behind.

"Oh, that's really nice," she said, parting her dressing gown, revealing her see-through nightie and knickers, " go all the way up my leg please that hurts too."

"I don't think I should, I'm sure your husband wouldn't approve."

"He's not here. He won't be home tonight, so do as you're told or I'll phone your employer then you'll be out of a job." She insisted on removing her nightie. "Come on, I want cream all over me, rub it in nice and gentle."

Not Guilty

James knelt on the floor and quietly removed his mobile, coughed twice and took two photos of her. After 10 minutes she sat up. "I want more around my breasts, especially on the nipples." He did as she requested. "I bet you'd like to fuck me, wouldn't you and I bet you've got a hard on," she grinned.

"I've never had sex with a woman so I wouldn't know what to do anyway so I'd certainly be boring for you. You need someone who is really experienced to please you."

"You haven't had sex?" Her smile broadened with anticipation, "You're still a virgin and how old are you?"

"I'm nearly 19."

"Sit by me." She said patting the settee.

She unbuttoned the top of his jeans and removed his penis, which was limp.

"I hope it gets bigger than that." She commented trying to arouse him.

She placed one of James's hands on her breast James started to become aroused. "That's better it's bigger than I thought it was going to be," she smiled.

She laid herself on the floor, parting her legs. "Come on then, I'll show you what to do my little virgin." She guided his penis inside her. "Come on, move up and down. Oh yes faster suck my breasts." After about an hour. "I can't stand any more. Get off, you're making me sore and you still haven't come." James quickly dressed himself and left.

The next morning when he returned to finish off the installation Mr Johnson was there. He came out to meet James.

"Son did she have any men here last night before you left."

"No, sir but I think you ought to see these two photos, she called me back last night saying I'd left tools on the stairs and she tripped and injured her ankle." James nervously showed him the two naked photos of his wife on the settee.

"Much as I suspected, I suppose she got you to sleep with her. Don't worry I'm not angry with you. I know it wasn't your fault."

James remarked, "I'm sorry sir, I didn't want to get involved, but she said she report me to my boss and I'd be dismissed. I do need a job Sir."

"I give £50,000 to anyone who could get rid of that bitch."

"Not a problem when I have the money in my hand. She will meet with an accident," James said very coldly.

Mr Johnson stared at him, "You're serious aren't you?"

"I wouldn't have said it if I wasn't. I don't like being treated like shit and I don't like liars."

"I'll have the money for you tonight in cash. If I divorced her, she'd take me to the cleaners."

"I'll get on with my work Sir we will talk later," James smiled.

"Yes thank you, young man, you just cured a headache for me, you must make sure I'm in London before you do anything."

"Of course."

James finished the installation and was about to leave the property when Mr Johnson pulled up in his Rolls-Royce. He passed a paper bag through the window to James. "Don't let me down son sooner the better please."

James nodded and drove off. He pulled over in the layby on the way back to London. There in the bag was £50,000. He just had to plan how to dispose of her and not be caught up in the murder. It would have to look like an accident whatever happened.

He allowed a week to pass then drove his own car because the van had a tracker fitted to Ross on Wye. He knew he could disarm the alarms by putting in a special code. He parked down in the town and walked the mile to the house. He could see the Rolls-Royce had gone, so her husband wasn't there. He climbed over the wall and deactivated the alarm on the side of the house.

Using a simple credit card he eased the front door open. He could hear a radio playing upstairs and someone splashing in the bath. He quickly went upstairs grabbing a small heater that had been left outside the bathroom.

He plugged it in and quietly opened the door; she was in the bath with another man. James hurled the heater into the water and they were both electrocuted. He moved the plug from the heater to inside the bathroom so it looked as if they'd been using it and it fell in the water by accident. He quickly ran downstairs and out of the front door and reactivated the alarms before climbing over the wall and removing his gloves.

He walked slowly along the road, making sure any car passing couldn't see his face. He jumped in his motor and drove back to London. Mission accomplished, he thought.

His boss phoned on Monday morning with directions to a job on the outskirts of Warwick. He was to meet a Mr Mercantile at the Rose and Crown pub 11 o'clock. James had to get his skates on to make it there in time. He finally pulled into the car park to find a man in a red Ferrari. The gentleman who got out was in his late 40s wearing a pinstripe suit. "You're the lad that deals with the intruder alarms?"

"That's right, sir, you have a problem in the pub?"

"No this isn't my establishment, come and sit in my car and I'll explain." He said, patting James on the shoulder. "I believe we have a mutual friend, Mr Johnson. He told me you did a marvellous job for him. So you've come highly recommended. I'd like you to get rid of something for me. Would you be interested?"

"I'm always interested in work I would like to see the job first if you don't mind."

"That's absolutely fine son, follow me in your van."

James followed. Not far out of Warwick they turned into a very plush residential area. None of the houses were worth less than a couple of million pounds each. Mr Mercantile introduced James to his wife. Jasmine, another peroxide blonde barely wearing any clothes, a right little stuck up tart. She left Mr Mercantile and James to discuss matters. "Do you see my problem?"

"Definitely, Sir."

"And here's my other problem, my daughter. Come with me young man we need to talk. Let's go into my office," he said placing an arm on James's shoulder and leading him in to a private office. "Shall we say a hundred thousand pounds for the two of them, but you can't do anything until I'm in Germany, which won't be for two weeks and I'm there for a month, so you have all that time to resolve the issue. How when and where I don't care just dispose of them. My wife's been seeing another man if not more. My daughters on her back for everybody she can get to screw her I want rid of them permanently."

"That shouldn't be a problem Sir I'd better just check your intruder alarm, I'm afraid I'll have to give you a bill, otherwise it will look suspicious and I can fit one of my special devices to deactivate the alarms when I decide to come."

Mr Mercantile smiled and shook James's hand. He removed a large packet from his desk drawer. James made some modifications to the alarm system and left, heading back for London. He'd finally found a business he enjoyed, although he wouldn't have considered it a few years back if events hadn't changed his life so dramatically.

Chapter 5
A New Career

James now had £150,000, which he hid very carefully in his flat. He wanted to buy himself a nice car, but new people would be suspicious and wonder how he could afford a luxury car. Two weeks quickly passed and he knew Mr Mercantile would be in Germany.

He drove across country to Warwick, avoiding all the roads with cameras on to avoid being tracked. It was 10 o'clock in the evening when he arrived outside the property. He could hear loud music coming from one of the bedrooms. He pressed his little fob and the alarms deactivated.

He must remember to remove the device before he left. He went round to the back of the house. There was a large tree shredder at the back. He could see Mrs Mercantile dancing in the dining room, which backed onto the rear garden. She was with a young man who was slowly stripping her.

James didn't expect to find her with someone so early in the evening although she knew her husband was abroad. James decided to take the frontal approach, wearing his gloves and taking out the handle of a pickaxe. He went round to the front, tried the door handle and it was unlocked. He entered quietly. He hid under the stairs, seeing the young man go into the bathroom. James seized the moment to open the door and hit him over the head. The young man dropped like a stone, and James shut the bathroom door.

Mrs Mercantile was standing naked looking through the windows James hit her from behind and she dropped immediately. He had brought some ties with him and secured her hands and feet. He then returned to the bathroom and did the same to the young man. Now there was just the matter of the daughter.

He quietly went upstairs although the music was playing, drowning out most of his approach. He peeped through one of the bedroom doors and could see Mr Mercantile's daughter sitting at the dressing table. James burst in and before she could move he'd struck her on the head.

She collapsed on the floor. He quickly tied her hands and feet, carrying her down the stairs into the dining room. He opened up the doors and laid her on the feeder into the shredder. He collected the other two, placing them on the in feeder. He went round and removed his device from the intruder alarm to make sure no evidence was left.

The only possible DNA from him would be on the pickaxe handle. He worked out how to start the shredder. The noise was horrendous and he fed the bodies straight through the machine and then switched it off.

There were hundreds of little pieces of quivering flesh lying in a pile. He quickly grabbed the pickaxe handle and returned to his car. alfway home he stopped on a bridge and through the pickaxe handle into the river.

He then continued home feeling proud of his self for a professional job well done. The police paid him a visit and when his boss found out he was immediately dismissed although James didn't really care he was all right for money for the time being.

James decided he needed a change of scenery purchasing a large static home on the outskirts of Stratford-upon-Avon for £20,000.

He would have to find new employment so went to sign on at the local job centre. He bumped into an old friend, Jackie. They looked at each other wondering whether to speak. James finally approached,

"How are you keeping?"

Jackie had blossomed into a beautiful young lady, "I'm fine. I just wish I could find a job. I have barely enough to live on, let alone buy new clothes", she complained.

"Do you fancy a coffee after I've signed on?" She smiled nervously, remembering their history.

"Okay, if you're sure."

James and Jackie jumped into his car and drove into Stratford. They parked in the multi-storey car park and made their way to a little coffee shop. There was some attraction there, but neither could understand what, considering he was going to kill her originally and she'd helped convict him, leading to a prison sentence.

James could not take his eyes off her beautiful shoulder length hair. She would push it back with the flick of her hand. He couldn't understand the way he was feeling about her, just didn't add up. One minute he wanted to kill her, the next minute he wanted to take her to bed.

Jackie finished a coffee, explaining she now lived in a hostel, she couldn't put up with her parents any longer. They continually moaned at her for not finding suitable employment and paying her way in the house. James reached across with his hand: "Come with me."

Jackie looked surprised and concerned at the same time. She nervously asked: "Where are we going?"

"Shopping," he said. She held his hand nervously, looking very confused.

"What are you short of in the way of clothes?"

"Shopping for me, why?" She paused, searching his expression for an answer.

"Don't ask so many questions," he smiled, tugging her hand.

They continued walking, looking in all the shops. James encouraged her into a shop for women's clothes. He stood there feeling rather embarrassed seeing bras and knickers and other garments draped everywhere.

He encouraged her: "Jackie, buy what you need, and I mean everything you need." One of the sales assistant came over to greet them at the door.

Jackie stared in shock at James's comment "Go and make yourself pretty Jackie, as if you need any improvement."

The sales assistant looked at Jackie: "You heard what the gentleman said." She smiled. Jackie just stared "How much can I spend, 20 quid?"

"There's no limit but could you manage on £1000?" James removed a wad of notes from his jacket. The sales assistant and Jackie gasped. "Don't buy rubbish Jackie, buy what you really want". The sales assistant commented: "I'll marry him if you don't". She laughed.

Jackie started shopping, selecting everything she felt she needed, trying not to spend too much. She mainly selected underwear and a couple of skirts and two new blouses.

James tried to conceal himself from the other females in the shop who seemed to look at him as if he was queer being in there.

Jackie's garments were placed in shopping bags. The total came to just over £400. James looked at her. "Is that all you want? You'd better take another look."

Jackie shook her head in disbelief. "Have you been drinking, James?" she smiled.

She selected a few more items which brought the total bill to £600. James counted the money out and paid, helping her carry the bags out of the shop.

"Why James, why thank you so much," she said, kissing him on the cheek and they returned to James's car. "What shall we do now?" he asked. "Would you like to see the place I bought?"

Jackie was feeling more comfortable. It wouldn't make sense for him to spend £600 on new clothes for her and then want to kill her. So, she agreed to go and look at his new place.

They drove just outside Stratford-upon-Avon parked outside the large static and went inside. "This is beautiful James," she said, looking in every room." James made the coffee they sat on the settee together. James explained what he'd been doing, but he did miss out the part of disposing of people. Jackie told him how horrible it was at the hostel and if you didn't lock your door you could have anybody walking on you.

James thought for a moment, although they just met, they did have history and his feelings for her were growing by the second. "Jackie, don't take what I'm going to say the wrong way please," he said, holding her hand. "If you really like to, and please be sure, you can live here with me and you can have your own room."

She thought for a moment, holding both his hands. "I think I'd be too scared to live with you James considering what happened the last time we met", she sighed.

"I'm not surprised at your answer, to be quite honest, I'm very attracted to you and I have no idea why?"

"Me too, James, and not just because you bought me new clothes I liked you when we were at school, but you never noticed me," She said, kissing him on the lips. They embraced for a short while. Then James made them both another coffee. "Would you at least consider going out with me Jackie until you feel you can trust me?" he said.

Her smile broadened. "Yes I would love to be your girlfriend."

She would have loved to have moved in, her mind was telling her one thing, and her heart another "Can I leave my new clothes here. I don't wanna take them back to that shit hole?"

"No problem."

James went and retrieved the carrier bags from the car, taking them into one of the bedrooms. "This can be your room until you feel safe and happy in yourself."

"Do you mind if I try my new clothes on I'm so excited," she smiled, jumping to her feet.

"Why not, knock yourself out girl." She kissed him again on the lips and embraced him before running off into the bedroom.

James sat on the settee quietly, drinking his coffee. Jackie called from the bedroom: "Would you like to see what you bought me?"

"Okay." She paraded herself several times in different garments she had selected, finally just wearing knickers and bra.

James smiled but did nothing else.

He just looked at her beautiful shape. Jackie approached him, taking him by the hand into his bedroom, releasing her new bra and removing her knickers. She slid herself into bed. James was unsure it was the right thing to do. He didn't want her to feel obligated because of the money he'd spent on her. "Are you sure? You don't have to Jackie, you owe me nothing."

She smiled, "I know James but I want to."

James undressed and nervously eased himself into bed. She caressed him and finally lay on top of him. They started to make love and stayed in bed for most of the day.

Jackie said: "Yes, I will live with you, I'm sure you'd never hurt me."

James responded: "Never, I just wanted to hold you and feel you close to me all the time." They kissed for a little while longer then dressed and went to the hostel and retrieved all her belongings, what few there were of them and returned to James's new property.

Chapter 6

Reinstated

James received a phone call out of the blue from his old employer, apparently his customers had been complaining and refusing to use his service because he had sacked James and they liked the service James provided.

James explained he was no longer in London but lived just outside Warwick. His old boss said he didn't care as long as he would work for him again because he was losing thousands of pounds. He would also give James a pay rise. He just couldn't understand why so many influential people were demanding he reinstate him."

Jackie commented, kissing James on the neck, "It's because you're such a lovely guy and you're all mine don't you forget it."

James went to London on the train and collected the works van. Tom shook him by the hand: "Thanks lad, you have some very powerful friends out there. I was almost going out of business until I agreed to give you your job back."

James's first destination was Ross on Wye to service Mr Johnson's alarm system. James phoned Jackie and explained he might be slightly later home than planned. He had a job to do on the way, which she was okay with. James arrived at the property, one he knew very well. Mr Johnson greeted him, patting him on the shoulder.

"It's lovely to see you again young man, you did a marvellous job on your last visit, couldn't wish for anything better, you saved me an absolute fortune, and I've recommended you to all my friends. Here's a little bonus for you."

Mr Johnson passed an envelope to James it contained £5000 in cash. "Thank you, sir, I'm glad to be of service." James checked the intruder alarm and drove back home. Jackie looked out of the window as he parked up in a brand-new van.

She ran out to greet him, kissing him softly on the lips. They went back inside and she prepared him something to eat. "James how much do you love me?"

"Now that is a silly bloody question Jackie." She placed his meal on the table. She did know what his reaction would be to the news "James I'm pregnant." She studied his expression he suddenly stopped eating got up from the table and scooped her up in his arms. "If you only knew how much I loved you, Jackie."

She was relieved he confirmed his love was solid for her and her unborn child. James gave her £1000. "You'd better get some baby gear together then love." Her smile broadened; she had made the right decision and chosen the right man for her. She kissed him tenderly, professing her love for him.

The next morning, he received a phone call to attend a job in Rugby; a Mr Jackson required his alarm system to be checked. James drove the 40 miles to Mr Jackson's property, another large mansion. Mr Jackson greeted him, a tall thin man in his late 50s.

Parked in the driveway was a Lamborghini a Ferrari and a Rolls-Royce. This guy was not short of money.

They shook hands. "You're the young man that's been recommended to me to fix a difficult problem with my alarm system. Let me show you my problem young man."

James followed him into the house, and was introduced to his daughter and what could only be described as a ponce of a boyfriend. Mr Jackson took James into his office. "You can see how attractive my daughter is and she's got herself involved with the bloody idiot he's taking her for every penny he can which is costing me a fortune. I would like him to disappear permanently, but please don't harm my daughter."

"I understand the situation entirely, sir. I need his address."

"That's the bloody problem. He shacked up with her here. I'm in London next month for a few days on business so that would be the best time for you to strike."

Not Guilty

Mr Jackson removed a package from under his desk. "There's £50,000! If you complete the task without hurting my daughter there will be another £50,000, well worth the money, considering what he's spending of hers."

"Very good, sir. I'll just make some adjustments to your alarm system and I'll be on my way."

Mr Jackson shook James's hand. "Thank you, son let's hope all goes to plan. Here are the dates when I'm away." He passed James a little note containing dates.

James made some adjustments to the alarm system so we could use his fob to deactivate the system when he returned. James was concerned this could be a tricky job; trying not to hurt Mr Jackson's daughter might be a problem.

James walked around the property so he could visualise in his mind where everything was, they had a swimming pool. He thought how nice and convenient it would be if the boyfriend drowned, but how would he separate Mr Jackson's daughter from her boyfriend?

James didn't want to involve Jackie in the slightest, or ask her to give him an alibi for that night. James explained to Jackie he had broken down with his van not giving any details of his location but assured her he would be home as soon as possible.

James had already disconnected the tracker on the van and he drove to Warwick. He then caught a bus to Rugby, just in case the van was spotted on camera, finally reaching the property. An hour later he turned off his mobile in case Jackie phoned.

Using his fob, he deactivated the alarms. A great stroke of luck, Mr Jackson's daughter and her boyfriend were in the swimming pool naked. He just needed to separate them. The boyfriend was sitting on the steps leading down into the pool, sponging the daughter's large breasts. James sat there watching the two for nearly an hour waiting for a miracle.

Finally, the phone rang in the house and the daughter went indoors and the boyfriend on his mobile stood on the top step of the pool. James stayed in the shadows, so he couldn't be seen from the flood lit pool coming up behind the boyfriend, grabbing the boyfriend's hair. He smashed his head against the edge of the pool, allowing the body to float, and if he wasn't dead from hitting his head he surely would be from drowning.

James quickly ran round to the side of the house, taking his device from the alarm system and exiting the property. He caught the last bus back from Rugby to Warwick driving home. The police never came to talk to him about what had taken place. It had been almost a month since he checked the alarm system.

The newspapers read: tragic accident, man slips hitting his head on the side of the pool and drowns. A week later, James received a phone call from his boss to return to Mr Jackson's property, there was another fault.

Mr Jackson came out to greet him with a broad smile. "You are a real professional and an artist. Thank God my friends told me about you, you saved me a lot of heartache."

Mr Jackson was as good as his word. He passed James another package and James gave him a bill for attending to his alarm.

"You can't beat good security." Mr Jackson voiced, smiling and seeing James off the property. James drove home slowly, with the horrible feeling he was being followed. He'd seen two cars in his mirror that he'd seen earlier in the day. He wondered how long it would be before he got caught. It was starting to become more than just a coincidence that at some of the jobs he attended, someone ends up dead a few weeks later. He could feel the noose tightening around his neck. He wondered what was the way out of the situation before he was caught. With the new baby on the way the last thing he wanted was to see his family from behind bars.

He would have to come up with a new way of dealing with people if another job came his way. James pulled over into a layby along the A46 just before reaching Stratford; the blue car went straight past and sure enough, a white one pulled in behind him, the same one he'd seen three or four times today with the same registration.

James drove off again, heading for home when he arrived he found Jackie in tears. She told him the police had been round questioning her of his whereabouts on certain nights. She said she couldn't tell them anything because she didn't know he was on call 24/7 and she never knew where he would be in the country.

James breathed a sigh of relief and reassured her there was nothing to worry about, but he knew in reality there was a lot to worry about and he must correct the situation quickly. He guessed his mobile phone would be monitored along with his computer.

Jackie mainly used the computer for online shopping. James burnt any evidence that could link him to any of the assassinations he had carried out.

Jackie had kitted out one of the bedrooms with all she would need for her new baby when it finally arrived and she had only three months to go. She was waddling around like a little duck.

James looked out of his front room window and saw a green car parked just beyond the entrance to the drive of the caravan park. He hoped the police wouldn't hang around long with all the cuts they were suffering to manpower and their budgets, unless they had found some evidence to implicate him and just needed a little more to shut the door on him.

The next five or six jobs were no problem at all. James knew he was being followed, but they were just run-of-the-mill jobs. It was almost as if someone high up knew he was under pressure and being followed.

After about six weeks he was no longer being trailed, they'd either given up or run out of funding and didn't have sufficient evidence to continue investigating him.

Jackie gave birth to an 8-pound boy, who they named Roger. She returned home three days later from hospital, a very proud mom. She hadn't bothered to contact her parents or any of her relations. She didn't want to have to explain her actions and why she became involved with James after sending him to prison. Life was starting to be good.

He'd taken maternity leave because he was entitled to, so he could help Jackie through the first few weeks. He enjoyed every moment, making sure she had every piece of equipment she could possibly want to make her task easier. She commented, "You know, I shall want another one in a couple of years." She smiled, feeding Roger.

James smiled. "I'll definitely enjoy that moment."

He then went out to the local jewellers and purchased an engagement ring. He came back home and after Jackie had put Roger to sleep, he went down on one knee and proposed to Jackie. The tears streamed down her cheeks. She was so overwhelmed and didn't expect it. "Yes, yes, I'll marry you, James, just let me regain my figure before we are married, please."

"I don't care what you look like Jackie you will always be beautiful to me."

James received a phone call from his boss. "Can you please handle this job for me, it's very important customer it's only in Cheltenham and they insist you attend."

James agreed, kissed Jackie goodbye and drove to Cheltenham to another very large mansion just on the outskirts down a very long drive. When he arrived, a Mr Dukes greeted him, another middle-aged man very smartly dressed and completely bald. He greeted James with a handshake and a big smile. "I have a serious alarm problem. Come with me and I'll explain."

James was escorted into the house and introduced to 2 females. "This is Claudette". James shook her hand, a very attractive brunette: "And this is Carla." Another very attractive young lady with jet black hair: "This young man is going to fix a security problem."

Mr Dukes led James into his private room, inviting James to seat himself in a large leather armchair. "Those two are my problem. They've been embezzling money from me for nearly over a year which has cost me 1.5 million, and I've decided enough is enough."

"That is not a problem to deal with, Sir," James responded.

Mr Dukes smiled, "I would also like the house destroyed. Everything is well insured so I will lose nothing. I will be in London next Tuesday all day. Could you possibly fit me in?"

"That shouldn't be a problem, Sir, I will come and fix your alarms next Tuesday morning, once I have the spare parts of course," James remarked.

Mr Duke shook his hand. "Wonderful, marvellous, there's £150,000. That should cover the problem." James made his usual modifications to the intruder alarm in case he needed to gain access. James left Mr Dukes and returned home.

The week passed quickly. Tuesday morning, James left the works van at home and went in his car to Stratford explaining to Jackie he wanted to do some shopping. Instead, he headed for Cheltenham, arriving at Mr Dukes's house.

Carla let him into the house. The minute she turned her back on him he placed his hand over her mouth so she couldn't scream. He put a knife to her throat and whispered in her ear. "One word and you're dead, do you understand?" She nodded.

He escorted her in to the study, taped her mouth and cable-tied her hands and feet. "Where is Claudette", he asked, pushing the knife against her throat and slightly moving the tape from her mouth. She said quietly, "In the shower." He replaced the tape over her mouth and quickly ran upstairs.

He could hear singing in the shower. He ripped the curtain away, thrusting the knife to her throat. She stared in horror as he held her arm helping her out of the shower, placed tape across her mouth and cable tied her hands escorting her downstairs to join Carla. Then he tied her ankles and laid her beside Claudette.

James thought to himself that he hadn't had sex for a long time, so why not enjoy himself while he was there. He cut the ties on Claudette's ankles and parted her legs. He started making love to her playing with her large breasts. Then he decided he ought to try the other one, and carefully removed her knickers and penetrated her.

He decided Claudette was the better of the two, so he re-entered her to finish off.

He now had to untie them and stop the moving or alerting anyone before they were engulfed in flames. He decided to electrocute them both. They should be no trace considering they were going to be burnt to a cinder. He removed the plug from the back of the computer, stripping the wiring, and attached it to Claudette. He nipped to the kitchen and came back with a bowl of water and threw it over them both. He then turned on the power supply after replacing the fuse with a higher voltage. They shook and jumped for a few moments and he left them connected to the mains for five minutes just to make sure they were dead.

He carried Claudette back upstairs to the shower and took Carla into the kitchen, removing all her ties as he did with Claudette, so everything looked natural. He went into one of the cupboards close to the gas cooker and with a spanner he released one of the joints so gas would leak. He ran upstairs as quickly as he could and ignited a portable electric fire. He left the premises in haste, heading for Stratford. He entered a jeweller to buy some earrings for Jackie and made sure he had a laugh and a joke with the staff there so they would remember him coming to purchase the earrings. He only spent £200, although he could have afforded a lot more but didn't want to give anybody any reason to question the cost.

James returned home and presented Jackie with the new earrings. She was over the moon, and hugged him. James sat down to watch the television, hoping to hear something about the fire and the loss of two lives. The 6 o'clock news hadn't mentioned anything about the fire. He turned on the radio, hoping to receive some information that way. There was nothing; he was starting to panic slightly when he remembered he hadn't removed his device from the alarm system before leaving, and he decided to go back; he could feel his palms turning sweaty.

He looked out of the window to see a police car draw up outside. They knocked on his door.

He invited the two officers in and Jackie said, "Will you never leave us alone?" James went over and placed his arm around his girlfriend's shoulder, "Don't get upset love their only doing their job".

The police officer smiled: "Can you give us your whereabouts today please, James?"

"Sure, I went shopping this morning for a present for my girlfriend." James passed them the receipt. "Then I came home after having a coffee and I filled my car up at the local garage, you can check with them. If you like, what's this all about officer?"

"A property you service the alarms on last week exploded today. Some of the pieces travelled over 200 yards, it was an absolute inferno. We are waiting for the fire brigade's report on the cause." "Excuse me for saying so officer I just want to do my job. I have a girlfriend I have a child. I want a normal life like anybody else. Why should I want to harm anybody or damage property?"

"You tell us James." The two officers left.

James smiled quietly to himself, knowing his plan had been a total success. His only concern was if they found the device he'd left on the intruder alarms to deactivate them, but he thought he could talk his way out of that one, simply by saying it saved disturbing the clients should the alarms go off while he's fixing the problem and he'd forgotten to remove it.

Chapter 7

Secret Service

Jackie decided she was now back in shape after the birth of her son Roger and she wanted to get married. They filled in the necessary paperwork, grabbing two people off the street as witnesses, and were married in the registry office.

Jackie was over the moon and so was James. They flew for a two weeks honeymoon in St Paul's Bay, Malta.

James had the sneaky suspicion they were being followed although he did suspect it could be imagination playing tricks on him. Roger was being grizzly, suffering from an upset stomach. Jackie said she would stay in the apartment with him and James could go for a quiet drink on his own.

He walked slowly down the narrow alleyway to the seafront when suddenly his path was blocked by a man in a suit in front of him and one behind. James was about to take a swing when the man from behind put a gun to his head. "I wouldn't do that James." The man removed his gun placing it back in his shoulder holster. "What do you want, I haven't got much money," James said, concerned.

"We don't want your money we just want to talk to you; come with us."

"Who are you? What do you want with me?"

A large van was parked at the end of the alleyway and he was escorted to it, the two men who got in with him were very smartly dressed. They drove a little distance and then he was taken inside what appeared to be a derelict building from the outside; on the inside it was very smart, with a couple of computers on desks and plush furniture.

James didn't know quite what to do he didn't want to get shot but he didn't want to be here either, and it was pretty obvious these guys meant business. They were obviously working for some organisation.

A middle-aged woman with a petite figure and blonde hair entered the room and sat behind a desk. "Don't be alarmed James we are not going to hurt you." James didn't reply. The woman continued, "We have been monitoring your activities and how you managed to dispose of people in a very efficient manner, in fact we are totally surprised at your professionalism considering you haven't been trained."

James went into a cold sweat feeling that this was the end of the road. "I don't know what you're talking about, I'm just a security engineer," he commented, hoping to bluff his way out.

The woman laughed and so did the two agents. The woman stood up in her dark grey suit perching on the edge of the desk, "We are not the police or terrorists. We are an agency working for the British government," she commented, tidying her skirt.

James commented quickly, "And I'm 007 James Bond pleased to meet you."

The woman got up from her desk walked over to James and held her hand out. "You can call me Mary." James shook her hand nervously, wondering what the hell he was going to do to get himself out of this situation. Mary continued, "We know what happened at Long Marston army camp and why. We also know you provided a service for several wealthy men and I will add you were very professional. We would like you to work for us."

"I already have employment thank you it doesn't pay very well but it's an honest job," James said standing up, "I'd like to go back to my wife and child. I'm supposed to be on honeymoon."

Mary returned to her desk sitting on the edge. "We actually own the company you work for." James dropped back down on the settee flabbergasted; he thought his heart was going to stop. "Tom is one of our agents, your boss." Mary poured a small glass of Scotch passing to James who had now gone as white as a sheet in shock.

"The only difference now instead of you deciding who will be eliminated, it will be us." She insisted with a broad smile. "Take him back John," she said looking at one of the agents. "We will talk again when you're back in the UK."

James stood up finishing his drink and shaking Mary's hand as he left the building with John who drove him back leaving him at the bottom of the alleyway to his apartment.

James was struggling to comprehend what had just taken place; it was almost a scene straight out of the movies, he thought.

He couldn't say anything to Jackie and place her in any danger. He entered the apartment and she greeted him with a kiss, "you've been drinking Scotch James?"

"Only a little one love do I taste good," he smiled, "how's Roger?"

"He settled down I think he'll be alright now I have given him a little medicine to try and settle his stomach."

"Good, let's hope we all get a good night's sleep," James professed, placed his arm around Jackie's shoulder as they walked to the bedroom.

The rest of the honeymoon was uneventful. James didn't see any signs of being followed. They finally flew back to Birmingham airport and drove the 25 miles back home.

The next morning James received a phone call to return his van to London. Tom said he had a new van for him, although he hadn't had this one very long he had decided to replace it with something better.

James drove to London returning the van to the yard. Tom greeted him and shook him by the hand "I hope you enjoyed your honeymoon son the work's been stacking up since you've been away. There's someone in the office who'd like to talk to you."

James went into the office. He couldn't see anybody in there; suddenly a back door opened, and standing there was Mary. She indicated with her hand for him to come in which he did without question. The room he entered was full of high-tech equipment. He followed Mary into another room. She invited him to sit down in the chair and she went round to sit at the desk. Mary smiled. "What we want you to do James is, when you attend to intruder alarm problems in certain properties, is to fit surveillance cameras and audio devices so we can monitor certain people's activity."

James exhaled. "So, I'm now a spy? Who am I really working for? And what happens if I get nicked, I don't want to go back to prison."

Mary smiled, "Who do you think stopped the police investigating you?"

"That's appreciated," James remarked smiling. "I suppose everything will be wonderful until you want to dispose of me then I'll end up in prison?"

"You been watching too many movies, James, you wouldn't be sitting here in if we didn't think we could trust you to carry out the assignments professionally."

James joked "Do I get danger money and a Ferrari?"

"No, you have a new van with better equipment. You can buy yourself a nice car with the money you've saved which I think is around £400,000 from your private ventures and no one will ask any questions. That doesn't mean you can break the law without express permission from me and me only do you understand me James," Mary said firmly.

James nodded in agreement. "And before you ask no you don't get a gun," she smiled. "I want you to carry this card with you at all times when you're at work if you are ever stopped by the police just show them this card they will leave you alone and I will kick your backside for being stopped."

James stood up and shook Mary's hand and her jacket parted slightly displaying her firearm strapped to her side. James left and went out into the yard. There, waiting for him, was a brand-new van. Tom approached him. "Be careful with this van James you will find it has far more power and we've modified the suspension for better cornering. It also cannot be detected by speed cameras but you can still be picked up by patrol cars so don't push your luck." James nodded in agreement.

Tom went round to the back of the van to open the doors. "In here you will find all the electronic equipment you will need: spy cameras, audio devices etc. The same as your old job, nothing has changed, only what you fit and where." Tom then returned to the front of the vehicle pointing to a key slot in the front wing. "When you leave the vehicle anywhere put your key in there and turn it once, it will electrify all the door handles."

"So we fry anybody you touches the van then?"

Tom smiled "No, they won't want to touch it again." Tom patted James on the shoulder, "Go home we'll be in touch and drive steady and get used to the vehicle, we don't want it bent. That reminds me," he smiled. "Don't disconnect the tracker, we're not stupid, there's two on every vehicle." Tom walked off laughing.

James sat in his new van and started the engine which sounded very powerful. He reversed out of the yard trying to drive slowly through London but the van just wanted to go. He could reach 60 miles an hour in first gear. He discovered on the motorway he could hit 130 miles an hour and backed off. He thought that was enough excitement for one day. He suddenly heard a voice. "Enough James, drive sensibly please." James searched the dashboard for a device and could see nothing. "Who's that?"

"Your boss Mary, this is your first warning I will not give you a second."

"Sorry Mary it won't happen again." James continued home. Jackie came out to see his new smart van commenting, "Look at the size of the exhaust pipe, it's as big as a drainpipe, whatever have they given you?"

Chapter 8

On the Road Again

James awoke to his phone ringing. It was Tom, instructing him to go to Bourton-on-the-Water to Mr Khan's house. He would receive further instructions on route. He was to be there by 10 o'clock. James had breakfast with Jackie, leaving her to deal with Roger when he woke up. James went out to the van and forgot to turn off the alarm system as he touched the door handle. He found himself shocked and sat on his backside. That was one hell of a kick, he thought. He turned the alarm off and drove steadily towards his destination. He heard Mary's voice: "James, I want you to fit listening devices all over the house, and a camera so we can see who enters the building, and I'd also like one in the living room if possible. I know it's going to be difficult, but do your best." The instructions ended.

James turned into the drive on the outskirts of Bourton-on-the-Water. It was quite a large house with lots of grounds and there were two Rolls-Royces parked on the drive, each having flags on the wings.

James rang the doorbell and an Asian gentleman answered: "You have come to fix my alarms?"

"Yes Sir, and install new ones so your house is more secure." The man smiled, displaying his white teeth through his tanned complexion.

"Good. I would be interested in any recommendations you have."

The gentleman showed him all round the house and James explained to him why he should have sensors in certain places and the advantages of doing so. Mr Khan agreed with all James's suggestions and left him with the work to complete.

James returned to the van and rang Mary on his mobile. "In the glove compartment, James, you will find a badge. Wear it so we can see around the property as you work." James attached it to his jacket. Mary confirmed it was working correctly. James placed everything he needed in his work bag and carried it into the house. The intruder alarm by the front door he switched for one with a camera, although you couldn't tell the difference. He also managed to locate an intruder alarm with a camera in the living room as Mary had instructed. James then went upstairs, to see two guards standing along the landing; they were both armed. They only watched James and didn't approach him.

He went to enter a room at the far end only managing to get the door slightly open but he did manage to catch a glimpse of a woman tied to the bed. A security guard slammed the door shut, pushing him out of the way, saying "No one is allowed in there." James was rather shaken.

Mr Khan heard the commotion and quickly attended the scene. The guards spoke to him in Arabic. Mr Khan's expression was one of concern. "What did you see when you opened the door?" he asked James.

"Nothing, I didn't get a chance, I was just going to fit an alarm in there."

Mr Khan patted James on the shoulder: "I'm sorry, that is my private room and no one is allowed in there, not even my wives."

James said, "Okay I'll leave it, to you sir."

Mr Khan pulled a wad of money from his jacket pocket thrusting it into James's hand, "You have done a good job."

"Thank you sir I'll collect my things and go, I've finished now."

"Good goodbye." Mr Khan disappeared into a room at the end of the landing. James quickly collected his things and returned to the van, removing his camera from his jacket and returning it to the glove compartment.

He started heading for home feeling he was lucky to escape. Mary said: "Well done James, you're the first person to gain access, the cameras are working beautifully and we can hear everything."

"Did you see that young woman tied on the bed?"

"Yes."

"Well what are you going to do about it, you can't leave her there".

"She is none of your concern, just forget you saw anything."

"That's ridiculous; what's he doing with her? Is she a captive?"

"It is none of your concern, James, go home and forget about it, leave the rest for us to sort out. You've completed your assignment." Mary never said another word.

James slowly drove home. He knew he shouldn't be concerned; after all he'd murdered a fair few women, so why should he be so bothered now what happened to one woman?

James stopped at a roadside cafe. Grabbing a coffee and a burger, he sat in the van drinking his coffee and eating his cheeseburger with extra onion.

Mary spoke: "Just so you don't do anything silly and we know you are likely to, the young lady you saw on the bed is one of our agents."

"That's great so you're just going to leave her there to have her throat cut?"

"No, we wanted proof she was there which you provided, now we will rescue her"

"If I'd had a gun I'd have shot those two guards and Mr Khan."

"And create an international incident, I don't think so James."

"Oh, I hadn't thought of that."

"That's why I'm the boss and you just do as you are told and leave the rest to me," she said firmly.

"Okay Mary."

"Good, now go home, come on now, we can monitor your every movement from here so I know when the vehicle is moving and it isn't so don't try and fool me. I don't want you anywhere near that house."

James laughed, "Okay mother." He heard Mary trying not to laugh and the line went dead.

James hadn't driven many miles before he saw blue lights flashing in his mirror. He pulled over and a police car drew up behind him. He wound down the window as a young policewoman approached him. "Just routine checks sir, could I see your driving licence and insurance."

"This is a works van officer; I was told by my employer to give you this card if I was ever pulled over."

James watched the colour drain from the policewoman's expression as she moved away from the van and contacted control. James heard her say, "Yes Sir immediately sorry sir my mistakes Sir." The young police officer returned the card to James immediately. James went to pass her his driving licence. "That won't be necessary you can go, sorry I inconvenienced you."

James could see the tears forming in her eyes, whoever she'd spoken to had put the fear of God in her.

James left the van and followed the policewoman back to her car. He asked politely, "Are you okay?"

"Yes sir I'm sorry I didn't realise who you work for."

James responded, "Don't worry, we all make mistakes, you're only doing your job." She smiled in appreciation of his comment.

James returned to his van and the police officer drove on in front. He continued home expecting Mary to contact him and burn his ears for being pulled over, she hadn't contacted him by the time he arrived home which was a relief.

James went inside picking up Roger from his playpen, giving him a big hug. Jackie made him a couple of sandwiches to tide him over until teatime.

At 11.30 in the evening James's mobile rang; he answered, the message was short "Get in the van and be quick." His phone went dead Jackie looked alarmed, "What's going on James?"

"Nothing to worry about love there's a short in the wiring on the job I did the other day and the alarm won't stop ringing I'll be as quick as I can."

James jumped in the van Mary spoke "James we have an emergency Miss Charleston has managed to escape Mr Khan's clutches; we want you to go and collect her and bring back to London as quick as you can. She will meet you at the garage she's injured and she needs attention immediately."

"I'm on my way."

"James, be careful. The people you are dealing with are terrorists and will not think twice about shooting you."

"You should have given me a bloody gun at least I could have defended myself," He protested.

"I know I'm going to regret this," Mary exhaled, "There is a firearm on board; if you are in any danger, go into the back of the van, press the red button behind your seat and you will find a handgun there but only use it if you have to James. We didn't expect you to be put in a position like you are I have no other agents in the area who can get there as quick as you."

James drove like the wind the van stuck to the road like glue he was hitting a hundred miles an hour most of the time. He cut across country through Chipping Camden and onto Stow, finally parking up at the disused garage on the main road on the outskirts of Bourton-on-the-Water.

He waited patiently, finally seeing Miss Charleston limping after running out of the hedgerow a little way ahead. He could see someone following her, he fired up the van and with rubber burning from the back tyres he charged down the road going straight past Miss Charleston and running over the terrorist, seeing the blood splatter up his windscreen. He turned the van around quickly and she climbed in and they sped off at high speed.

Miss Charleston was holding her leg, she'd been shot. James pulled over under a street light in Stow-on-the-Wold. He quickly grabbed the first aid box from behind the passenger seat, handing it to Miss Charleston.

She smiled. "Thanks for coming to rescue me, I thought I wasn't going to make it for a while" She bandaged her leg quickly. James headed for the motorway to London as he'd been instructed to bring Miss Charleston back to headquarters.

Her skirt had been torn and so had her blouse, she looked as if she'd been dragged through a hedge backwards. Mary spoke: "Juliet, are you okay?"

"I'm shot in the leg Mary, but will make it back. James ran over one of the gunmen though, to stop him shooting me again." Juliet smiled in appreciation.

"Well done James, we will have to train you to use a gun, although we thought it would never be necessary. You should be with us according to the tracker in the next half hour. We will be waiting."

"Thank you James, they would have killed me if you hadn't come to my rescue," Juliet confirmed.

"You're welcome. I wanted to go back to get you out before, Mary wouldn't let me."

"I'm glad you saw me and the agency knew where I was."

James pulled into the yard. People were swarming everywhere as he got out. Juliet was taken away to have her injuries attended to and be debriefed. James went into the office, looking back through the window he could see his van being cleaned from top to bottom. Mary invited him into the office: "Your performance was outstanding James, we made the right decision with you."

Mary poured a small glass of Scotch from her decanter and passed to James: "You didn't hesitate, James, you took care of Juliet without thinking twice. You are a natural assassin."

James turned round to see a monitor on the wall displaying the carnage he'd left behind. Police cars were everywhere by the old garage. James commented, "I must phone Jackie, she'll wonder where I've got to."

"Taken care of, James." James looked alarmed. Mary smiled, "Don't worry, we sent Jackie a text message from you saying the repairs were going to take a little longer than you thought, and she should go to bed and not worry."

"She will realise that wasn't my number."

Not Guilty

Mary shook her head smiling showed James a device that had a lot of mobile numbers displayed. "We simply select the mobile number and send the message to whoever we want from whoever we want."

James placed his glass on the table, stood up, went round and kissed Mary on the cheek. She stared at him rather surprised by his action. "That is inappropriate behaviour James," she said sternly. "The van is ready, you can go home." She smiled. "We've had an agent watching your premises just in case Khan linked you to his brother's death."

James glanced back before leaving the office and winked at Mary she tried not to blush "Go home James please."

James steadily drove home arriving home at daybreak. Jackie looked out of the window and ran out to greet him. They both went inside and Jackie made him some breakfast insisting he should go to bed and rest.

A whole week passed; no phone calls, no callouts. James wondered if this was the lull before the storm; he couldn't imagine Mr Khan allowing his brother to be killed without any reprisals.

James was summoned to the office and received a day's training on how to use a handgun should the occasion arise. Much to his surprise Juliet appeared at the firing range just using a walking stick while she recovered from her injury.

She showed James various techniques to help make sure he hit the target he wanted to, either a kill shot, or just a wound. Juliet offered to take James for a coffee before he went home. James climbed into her BMW and she took him into town to a Riverside Café, taking an outside table looking out over the river.

Juliet commented sipping her coffee. "Kissing Mary on the cheek is a no-go area," she smiled, "Her husband was killed in action; he was an agent."

"Oh," James replied, "it was only a thank you peck."

Juliet smiled. "She was quite amused actually and shocked."

Juliet had beautiful long black hair and dark brown eyes and a lovely figure, James thought to himself, what is a beautiful girl like this doing working for the agency?

"Would you like something to eat Juliet?"

"No, thanks I'll just pile on the pounds," she smiled.

They continued to talk for a while. Juliet was interested in his family life and how he'd become involved with the agency. She returned him to the yard where his van had been refuelled and checked over by Tom and the mechanics to ensure the vehicle was in perfect working order.

James took the liberty of kissing Juliet on the cheek. She looked at him surprised. "Do you kiss every female you meet?" "Only the pretty ones," he smiled, seeing Mary looking through the window grinning and shaking her head slowly.

James headed for home feeling rather pleased with himself; he'd learnt a new skill, how to use a handgun properly, which he thought may save his life one day. Mary spoke through the intercom in the van: "James, return to the yard immediately please." No explanation was given and Mary didn't sound very happy, so he turned the van round at the next junction and headed back for London. He pulled into the yard; everyone was looking at him strangely.

He walked into the office. Juliet and Mary were waiting for him. They all went into Mary's office. "Sit down James please." Juliet sat beside him on the settee. Mary sat behind a desk. Juliet held James's arm. James knew something was really wrong. Mary spoke, "I have some bad news James, Jackie has been shot." James jumped to his feet; Juliet pulled him back down. "Let me finish, she's only been wounded in the shoulder, Roger is fine, unharmed."

"Where, how, who by? I'll kill them!" James shouted with tears running down his cheeks. His very soul was being torn apart with unbearable pain.

"One of Kahn's associates trying to inflict pain and suffering."

"Jackie was walking along the driveway and before John our agent had chance to intervene Jackie had been shot in the shoulder. John did shoot the other person but he got away in a car."

Juliet placed her arm around James's shoulder and hugged him.

"Where's Roger?" James asked quickly.

Mary looked at her watch. "He should be coming through this door in the next five minutes with John. Our other agents are clearing up the mess and the local police have been made aware this is a code red situation."

Mary moved over and sat the other side of James, "I'm really sorry, we should have made you move to a safe place, although we heard nothing to indicate Khan had connected you to his brother's death."

"You know I'm going to kill him Mary," James said calmly. Mary watched his face turn to stone, an expression she had never seen before, but knew he meant every word of his last sentence.

"It's already been taken care of James, his body is presently being flown back to his country of origin after a tragic road accident."

Mary watched the colour returned to James's face. John entered the office carrying Roger, who seemed oblivious to the whole situation. Before James could rise to his feet Juliet had taken Roger from John's arms and was cuddling him very tightly kissing him on the cheek, she then reluctantly passed him to James.

Mary stood surveying the whole situation. James looked across to John: "Thank you."

John remarked, "I'm sorry James I tripped on a barbed wire fence where I was hiding, if I'd only been a few seconds quicker Jackie wouldn't have been shot."

James could see the gash on John's leg through his ripped trousers. Mary said, "John go and have medical attention." He nodded and went out of the office.

Mary's phone rang. As she answered her original relieved expression drained from her face. James and Juliet gazed towards her, wondering what the problem was.

Mary put the phone down. "James, it appears the bullet was laced with poison. Jackie has been moved to a secure unit. We have the antidote but it will take some time for her to recover," she commented with watery eyes.

Tom knocked on the door and entered. "I've fitted a car seat in Juliet's BMW so it's safer for Roger to travel back home."

James quickly commented. "Why didn't you put it in the bloody van?"

Tom looked to Mary for an answer; he'd done as he'd been instructed by Mary.

"It could take up to 3 months for Jackie to recover, James. I'm assigning Juliet to look after Roger and you while she is still incapacitated to some degree."

Mary sat behind a desk. "I will go and see Jackie myself and try and explain what's gone on when she becomes conscious again, but it's most likely she will be unconscious at least for a month."

Juliet carefully removed Roger from James's arm. Roger smiled feeling very secure in her arms.

"I want to see Jackie," he said firmly.

"There's no point James she's unconscious; you will be notified as soon as she comes round." Mary said standing up continuing, "Juliet, take care of these two, I'm relying on you."

Juliet smiled and nodded remarking : "Come on James I'll follow you home."

Juliet strapped Roger in the back of her BMW in the newly fitted car seat. Mary watched from the window with a very concerned expression; she obviously wasn't telling the whole story of what she knew and what may lie ahead. James headed for home, Juliet closely followed. By the time they'd reached the static home, Roger had fallen asleep. Juliet carefully carried him in, lowering him into his cot. She quietly closed the door removing her jacket and started to make something to eat finding her way round the kitchen, searching for various items.

James looked out of the window towards the main road to see a patrol car parked up. James suspected there was far more to this situation than anyone was letting on. He just hoped he was not being used as bait for Kahn's associates to seek revenge. He was not so worried about himself but he didn't want Roger involved at all if that was the case.

Juliet had not removed her firearm which was attached to her belt around the waist. James enquired "Do you sleep wearing a gun?"

Juliet smiled, "Do I make you nervous? you have nothing to worry about James, no one will get past me," she reaffirmed.

"So you are expecting trouble?"

Juliet folded her arms and turned to face James. "We don't know; they've obviously connected you to Kahn's brother's death somehow."

"So the agency is using me as bait and Roger, I think that's bloody disgusting," he said frostily.

Juliet sat beside him on the settee. "No, Mary would never place you in danger or Roger, we're just being careful," she commented, patting him on the leg, getting up to make the coffee and returned with two mugs. Juliet removed her gun from the holster and attached a silencer James looked on rather puzzled. Juliet smiled. "I don't want to wake Roger or the neighbours if I have to shoot someone."

James almost choked on his coffee at her comment. "That's really considerate," he smiled. Continuing, "Have you had to shoot many people Juliet?"

"Only a dozen or so," she replied without a hint of remorse and joked, "especially men who kiss me without my permission."

"I'm sorry I kissed you the other day, I didn't mean to offend you."

"You didn't I'm a black belt in judo you'd have been on your arse if I was offended," she said firmly, continuing, "So is Mary."

James tried to make light of the situation. "I'm a black belt to keeps my trousers up!"

Juliet smiled, standing up and moving to the window and scanning the area; then returning to the kitchen, serving up the meal she had made. They sat quietly eating, occasionally glancing up at each other, wondering what the other was thinking. James was concerned about Jackie and the situation he'd placed in through his own stupidity. Juliet heard Roger, starting before James could move, she was on her feet attending to him; he seemed to take to Roger as if she was his natural mother.

Chapter 9

Destination Unknown

James went into the bathroom, looked in the mirror and decided it was time to lose the beard. He hadn't seen his face for so long he couldn't remember what it really looked like without a beard. After managing to cut himself several times with the razor, he finally had a clean face apart from pieces of toilet roll stuck on the cuts to stop the bleeding.

He returned to the living room. Juliet stared. "Whatever made you do that? You look like you've been in a battle already," she laughed.

"I thought I should change my appearance, it may confuse any assassins," he said, pulling the pieces of toilet paper from his chin.

"Who's a handsome man, I'd only just got used to you with the beard," she said, walking over to have a closer look.

James blushed. Juliet laughed at his embarrassment.

"You can have my bedroom tonight Juliet I'll sleep on the settee."

"No, I won't I'm staying out here. My orders are to protect you and Roger so don't argue," she said firmly.

James looked in on Roger, he was fast asleep. "I'm going to bed then, Juliet, just help yourself to anything you want; let's hope tomorrow is a better day," he said with a sigh.

Juliet smiled and nodded. James returned from his bedroom with a duvet and a couple of pillows and placed them on the settee. Juliet smiled. "Thank you."

James went into his bedroom lying on his back looking to the ceiling then turning his head to see no Jackie beside him. He knew he wouldn't get much sleep, the bed seemed empty and strange. He could hear Juliet on her mobile talking to Mary who was obviously checking up on her to make sure everything was okay. James eventually fell asleep. He awoke hearing Roger and Juliet playing in the front room.

He sat up in bed listening to the way she was playing with Roger and talking to him. She couldn't have had much sleep on the settee all night he concluded. James dressed and went into the front room to see Juliet, just tidying up after feeding Roger and changing him.

James commented "You're going to make someone a wonderful wife and you'll be a great mother one day."

Juliet glared at him. He almost felt she was going to shoot him for the comment. He sat down to eat the breakfast she'd prepared for him and decided not to question her lack of response to his last comment.

James suggested. "Let's all go into town and take Roger to the park, it looks like it's going to be a nice day."

Juliet didn't respond other than saying "We'll go in my car." She placed Roger in the car seat and they drove to the park a few miles away. Juliet had removed the silencer from her gun so it would fit in the holster and could be hidden beneath her jacket. James wondered how he could have possibly offended her with his comment concerning marriage and having children. It had obviously upset her considerably because her attitude had changed and he didn't know why.

Juliet held Roger as if he was her own, she would place him in the swing and gently push him. James sat on the edge of the slide watching the two of them play together which seem to make Juliet extremely happy. Occasionally, she would look up and across to him and then survey the field for any signs of unwanted presents.

A stranger came across starting to talk to Juliet he placed his hand on her shoulder and within seconds he was on his back with her foot resting on his throat. She lifted Roger from the swing before he could stand up and walked towards James. The stranger struggled to his feet and walked off quickly holding his throat.

He joked, "Was he chatting you up?"

Juliet glared at him and placed Roger in the sandbox. "All bloody men are the same," she said angrily.

He carefully placed his arm around her shoulder. "Come on, tell me what's happened to you to make you the way you are." James eased her down onto a nearby swing seat and he sat beside her.

Juliet explained she'd been sexually assaulted by her father. She took a knife from the kitchen and stabbed him to death at the age of 15. Her mother had disowned her, blaming her for encouraging her father by the way she dressed. She'd been placed with foster parents and then joined the agency at the age of 18. James exhaled, "Oh shit that must have been awful."

Juliet rested her head on his shoulder, obviously feeling safe; she was a force to be reckoned with, and no one would ever hurt her again, she'd made sure of that by her training. "You're the first person I've told, James, other than Mary and I know what happened to you. Mary told ne you had your life ruined too, although I'm surprised you married one of the girls who put you in prison."

"It wasn't really Jackie's fault, she was being bullied by Jennifer, and when I met her again we sort of fell in love - strange how things turn out!"

Juliet patted James on the leg, "Come on, you can buy lunch, I'm starving," she smiled, walked over to the sandbox picking up Roger and brushing the sand from his clothes.

Roger would smile every time Juliet picked him up and he would always place his arms around her neck for security.

They went into town to a local restaurant that provided a high chair for Roger. Juliet was relieved she had explained her feelings and behaviour to James; they were kindred spirits, each suffering at the hand of someone else's deception. James thought watching Juliet feed Roger, if he hadn't married Jackie, he certainly would have wanted Juliet. Her behaviour was similar to Jackie's; they could have been twins he concluded.

They returned home and Juliet lowered a very tired Roger into his cot. She returned to the living room, removed her coat and flopped on the settee, while James made her a coffee. James commented, "Were just like an old married couple," he laughed. Juliet smiled. "I'm knackered; children wear you out although I wouldn't miss this assignment for all the tea in China."

James suggested she go and rest on his bed for a few hours' sleep it would be another long night. She agreed and went into James's room taking her suitcase so she could change. James could hear her snoring after about an hour which rather brought a smile to his face. He would definitely have to rib her about that later on.

James quietly opened the bedroom door after hearing her stop snoring and peeped in; her gun was already pointing straight at his head, her reaction was quick. "Sorry if I startled you Juliet when you stop snoring I was concerned, just checking you're okay."

"I don't snore," she scolded. James closed the door and returned to the settee, watching the television quietly, trying not to disturb anyone. James remembered he had a gun in the back of his van. He grabbed the keys and went quietly out of the static home trying not to disturb anybody. He retrieved his gun and that was the last thing he remembered, until he found himself in Juliet's arms. She was mopping his brow where a bullet had grazed just missing the target which was him.

Juliet helped him back into the static home. She had already phoned Mary telling her of the event and Mary confirmed the assassin was over 2 miles away on a hill and had been eliminated by another agent from a helicopter. Mary had instructed Juliet not to leave James under any circumstances or let him out of her sight. This was confirmation the terrorists were really after James for his part in Khan's assassination.

"You bloody fool James," Juliet scolded, still not properly dressed, only in a T-shirt and pants. She'd heard the bullet hit the back of the van.

"What happened," James asked holding his forehead.

"A sniper 2 miles away on the hill over the back took a shot at you. Mary is absolutely fuming with me, I should have never let you talk me into having a snooze."

"I'm going around Khan's house to shoot the bloody lot myself, I'm not sitting here and be used the target practice," he said, frustrated.

Juliet placed a bandage around his forehead, feeling her heartbeat increase the closer she came to him. She leant forward, securing the bandage behind his head; when she'd finished she slapped his face. "Stop looking down my T-shirt," she scolded, trying not to smile.

He pulled away "I wasn't, well not really." They both sat there for a moment on the floor looking into each other's eyes, understanding each other's feelings yet trying to stay professional.

Juliet helped James to the settee and she went into the bedroom to dress herself. Luckily Roger had slept through the whole incident and was oblivious to what had taken place.

Juliet returned wearing her jeans and blouse and went off to make them a coffee. James's mobile rang; Mary had phoned to give James a royal roasting for his stupidity although she was relieved he hadn't been killed.

She also made it very plain he was not to go anywhere without Juliet until she was convinced the threat no longer existed to any of her agency staff. Juliet could tell by the expression on James's face Mary was not happy.

Mary asked to speak to Juliet. James passed the phone over. "Hi Mary, I'm not sleeping with him I'm sleeping in the front room." Mary had instructed Juliet to be in the same room at all times. She was not only concerned James would go on a manhunt without having the experience to do so but there may be another attempt on his life.

She informed Juliet, Jackie was not responding to treatment as well as they'd hoped and it was quite possible she may die and under no circumstances was she to make James aware of how grave the situation was. Mary rang off.

"What was that about," James enquired, "who's sleeping with whom?"

"Oh, nothing, she just doesn't trust you she thinks you'll go on a killing spree."

"How's Jackie, did she say?"

"No, she didn't comment on Jackie." Juliet commented, feeling rather guilty for not telling him the truth.

There was a knock at the door. Jackie pulled her gun from its holster and peered out of the curtain to see who was standing there. Juliet could see it was a policewoman. She returned her gun to its holster and opened the door. The young policewoman asked if she could come in. Juliet stood aside placing her hand on her gun; the young police officer saw the firearm and the badge. She nervously stepped inside removing her hat. James suddenly realised it was the same young police officer who'd pulled him over before. He smiled, "I've seen you before, what have I done wrong this time?"

Juliet watched intently not removing her hand from her gun.

"Nothing Sir," she said nervously. I heard your wife had been shot and I knew you had a young child and I just wondered if I could be of any assistance when I'm not on duty." The young officer played with her hat. James stood up. "That's very kind of you to even think about me and my son. Juliet is here to assist me but thanks all the same for the offer."

"I'll go then, sorry I troubled you." She smiled and left.

"Looks like you have an admirer, James," Juliet commented, watching the policewoman walk down the road to her car.

James had a serious headache and decided he would go and lie down. Juliet locked the front door and came into the bedroom with him. James

Not Guilty

slid into bed only removing his trousers and jumper Juliet lay on the bed fully clothed with her gun resting on her stomach. James woke up to find Juliet on her side with her head against his. She stirred and quickly moved herself to her original position. James asked, "You okay Juliet?"

"Yes of course," she said sliding off the bed and stretching, placing her gun back in its holster.

They both heard Roger giggling and chattering in his own language. They both smiled then realised the sounds were coming from the living room. Juliet open the bedroom door with her gun poised expecting to find an intruder. Sitting in the armchair playing with Roger was Mary. Juliet holstered her weapon, looked back to James, indicating with her hand to come quickly. James jumped out of bed and they both entered the living room like guilty children. Mary glared at them both. "Juliet you snore I could have taken Roger and neither of you would have known."

"I locked the front door," Juliet protested at the accusation she'd been negligent.

Mary shook her head slowly, looking over her glasses which Roger took pleasure in trying to steal. "No terrorist is going to knock, they can pick a lock just like you or me. Juliet, you should know that, or were you so intent on getting James into bed?"

Juliet folded her arms and was about to shout. Mary placed her finger to her lips. "Stay calm in front of Roger. Coffee, please."

James protested: "Juliet didn't sleep with me, she lay on the bed." He moved to put the kettle on.

Mary smiled. "I know, James, I looked in on you both before attending to Roger who was playing in his cot."

Mary passed Roger to Juliet, "He needs changing." Juliet went into Roger's bedroom to change him. Mary moved over to where James was making the coffee, placing her arm around his shoulders. "James, Jackie isn't doing very well," she said quietly. Continuing, "we really are doing all we can for her. I think you should come and see her, even though she is still unconscious."

Juliet returned to the living room in time to see James kiss Mary on the cheek again. Mary pulled away and stared at him: "Please stop doing that James, it is inappropriate."

"Thank you for being honest Mary, where is Jackie?"

"She's in London in our secret facility. I will have to take you, otherwise they won't let you in, and if you keep kissing me, you will end up in there yourself." Juliet turned her back on them both trying not to laugh at Mary's comment. She could see from the expression on Mary's face she'd enjoyed every moment of the attention.

Mary said calmly "There'll be a helicopter waiting for us in the field beyond, in the next 20 minutes. You come with me James; Juliet stay here with Roger and look after him, if you can stay awake long enough?"

Juliet protested. "I think Roger should see his mother just in case you know what I mean Mary."

Mary sat down, sipping her coffee in thought. "Yes we'll all go, it makes sense." Mary knew exactly what Juliet was getting at, it could be the last time Roger would see his mother alive, and James his wife, for that matter."

Juliet changed Roger's clothes into something warmer and they made their way across into the adjacent field, as they heard the helicopter approaching. Juliet placed her hands over Roger's ears to shield him from the noise, although he seemed very excited about the whole situation, not understanding what was really going on.

They arrived in London, landing on top of a hospital roof. There were several soldiers carrying rifles, monitoring everyone as they descended into the building. They were guided through to where Jackie was lying with more tubes in her than Battersea Power Station.

James bent down and kissed Jackie on the forehead, taking Roger from Juliet and being careful not to let him play with the tubes. Roger patted her forehead with his hand, saying "Mum." The doctors watched, concerned, then without warning, Jackie opened her eyes. The doctors pushed past everyone; Jackie had gained consciousness, which was a good sign. Roger started to cry, becoming frightened of the situation he didn't understand.

Juliet retrieved Roger from James and he stopped crying, feeling more secure with her than anyone else at the moment.

James quickly held Jackie's hand. She squeezed gently.

"Don't, worry Jackie love, you're safe here, no one will hurt you, I promise you."

Juliet turned away with tears in her eyes, pleased Jackie had regained consciousness and realising her mission would soon be over, probably never seeing James again. James kissed Jackie on the forehead promising to return soon to see her.

Mary ordered Juliet and James to use the helicopter and return home, she would make her way back to the office. The journey home was very silent, the only person making a sound was Roger, enjoying the whole experience, pointing to the lights below as they flew over the city. They landed an hour later in the field just beyond the caravan park, returning to the static home.

A neighbour approached, a retired sergeant from the Coldstream Guards. "James, an electrician called in to replace your fuse box I sent him away telling him you weren't in although we did look around the outside of your home." James patted the guy on the shoulder.

"Thanks mate." They waited till he gone out of sight Juliet commented.

"Did you order an electrician?"

"No, I'd fix it myself, we'd better not go anywhere near until we establish if a bomb has been planted," he said carrying Roger. Juliet phoned Mary; she immediately dispatched a team to investigate and instructed Juliet to phone for a taxi and go to a hotel for the night until it was established what had gone on while they were away.

James commented "I wouldn't have thought they'd have been so persistent, I only killed one of them and I wouldn't have thought that was such a big deal."

"It's because you killed Khan's brother and we killed Khan; there are three other brothers somewhere and they want revenge."

The taxi finally arrived, taking them into Stratford-upon-Avon where they went into the Falcon hotel, booked a room for the night and had a meal served in the room.

At 6 o'clock in the morning Juliet's phone rang. Mary informed Juliet that a package had been removed from under the static home with a timer set for midnight and it was now safe to return home. Luckily Juliet had placed three spare disposable nappies in her handbag.

She washed and changed Roger and they returned home. Somehow the terrorists were receiving information of everyone's whereabouts; there was obviously somebody on the inside of the organisation. Mary had contacted Juliet again, advising her and James to be extremely vigilant until they discovered the mole in the organisation. She also decided there was no point in trying to take them to a safe house because if there was a security breach they would be no safer there than where they were now.

James decided to take matters into his own hands, telling Juliet he was just nipping into town to buy a couple of bottles of wine. She looked at him rather suspiciously and told him not to be long. James immediately headed for Bourton-on-the-Water after finding the two tracker devices on his van and isolating. He suspected the brothers if they were in the country would be there in hiding.

Broad daylight was not the ideal time to go snooping around the property, however he had shaved his beard off and perhaps that may just give him the edge. He removed his gun and holster, attaching them to his waist, checked the gun was fully loaded and he had a spare box of shells in his jacket pocket.

He decided he would go in with all guns blazing and sod the consequences. He turned his mobile off so Juliet or Mary could not contact him. He rang the doorbell. One of the security guards answered. James shot him dead on the doorstep; another guard came running down the stairs and James shot him in the head. James ran upstairs and kicked each door open, checking there was no one inside. In the far room along the landing where he'd originally seen Juliet. There were three men; he didn't hesitate and fired a bullet into each of their heads.

Mary couldn't contact him although she could see every movement he made around the house and how he executed everyone in there without hesitation.

He quickly reloaded, carefully walking down the stairs, checked all the other rooms and discovered in a cupboard under the stairs, a stack of boxes filled with explosives. He quickly reversed his van to the front door, slid the dead guard out of the way and loaded the boxes of explosives into the van, remembering on one job he'd released the gas pipe in order to cause an explosion that could easily be explained away.

He went into the kitchen and released a locking nut until he could hear the gas escaping. He ran upstairs, cutting a wire on an electric appliance, causing an arc. Once the gas reached the spark he thought it would be good night Vienna for the property.

James closed the front door and drove very slowly towards home. Mary started ranting and raving at him over the intercom at his stupid actions and what the consequences could have been. Her final comment was: "We saw everything you did on camera, a brilliant disposal and elimination, although I didn't authorise it."

Not Guilty

When James arrived home he found Juliet had put Roger to bed; she turned on her heels and slapped him across the face very hard. "How dare you lie to me, Mary phoned and told me what you've done, you stupid, irresponsible idiot." She went to strike him again and he grabbed her wrist with his free hand. He grabbed her waist, pulling her to him and kissing her on the lips. She pulled away in shock, realising he did have feelings for her like those she had for him.

James rubbed his face where she'd struck him. Mary phoned James's mobile. "Hi Mary" James said, "have you cooled down, I have several boxes of explosives in the van I would like to get rid of."

"I know, James, they will be collected shortly by one of our operatives," she said firmly, continuing, "You must not let your heart rule your head, you must follow my instructions, you understand me, James?"

"Okay mom."

"Don't be so bloody rude James, I'm not amused." Mary rang off.

Juliet was laughing. "Don't push her to far James she won't tolerate it."

James shrugged his shoulders. "She loves me really," he smiled.

Chapter 10

Who is the Mole?

Mary had been in to see Jackie, who was making a slow but positive recovery. Mary had explained to her what had happened and who James was working for. Jackie was rather upset because she thought James should have trusted her to keep a secret considering she was now his wife and the history they had together.

Mary phoned James and explained the conversation she had with Jackie. Juliet listened to the conversation. Mary estimated according to the doctors' information, it would be another month before Jackie could come home. It was imperative they find the leak in the organisation, not only to protect Jackie from another attack but also the security issue for any of the agents.

James made a coffee, passing one mug to Juliet as they sat on the settee together. "How are we going to find the mole?" James remarked; continuing "I must go and see Jackie today, would you like to come with me?"

Juliet was silent for a moment. "Okay unless you really want to be on your own with her, I don't want to be in the way," she commented with a heavy heart.

"You're my partner, you're never in the way, and Roger worships the ground you walk on. He likes you better than me or his mother."

Juliet smiled. "I will miss him when I'm reassigned," she sighed heavily.

James placed his arm around Juliet shoulder he could feel her trembling; he didn't know whether it was fear or preparing to strike in defence.

"Don't, James please," Juliet said calmly standing up and moving away from him, looking through the window watching the cars on the main road.

James walked over and stood behind her, "I'm sorry Juliet I didn't mean to upset you I'm a bit thoughtless sometimes."

She turned to face him with tears in her eyes. He gently placed his hand behind her head, encouraging her to rest her head on his shoulder, and kissed her fragrant hair. They stood there for several minutes, no one said a word, then Juliet pulled away. "I'm a silly bitch, let's go to London and see Jackie," she said drying her eyes.

They drove to London, Roger in his car seat chattering away to himself. On their arrival the hospital was in total lockdown; something had happened. Military personnel were everywhere.

Juliet showed her badge and she was allowed to drive in. Mary came out to greet them both with tears in her eyes. James jumped out of the car and much to everyone's surprise, Mary embraced him. Juliet removed Roger from the car seat, trying to assess the situation and Mary's action.

They went inside quickly into a private room. Mary dabbed her eyes trying to compose herself. Juliet had never seen Mary shed a tear in the eight years she'd known her. Mary sighed heavily. "We have the mole, in fact there were two of them. One was Tom my second-in-command in the organisation and the other was a young policewoman who pulled you up on the way back from Bourton-on-the-Water, if you remember, we have her in custody."

James smiled. "That's great news and you finally realise you are in love with me he," joked.

Juliet said. "Be quiet James there's more to this than meets the eye, let Mary finish."

Mary swallowed hard and sighed "I'm afraid Jackie is dead she had a massive heart attack and they couldn't save her after Tom increased her medication to a level her body couldn't stand, and it was too late before the doctors realised what had happened."

James cried broken hearted. "What was he doing here Mary?"

"Tom had clearance to go anywhere James, he was my second-in-command." She continued: "He was also a relation of Khan's, which we've only just discovered. The young policewoman was one of his daughters."

Mary looked across to Juliet. "Take him home and stay with him, he's going to need your support."

"Of course I'll do whatever I can Mary," she said, cuddling Roger.

James and Juliet drove home, Roger in his car seat, still oblivious to what had taken place. James didn't know how he was going to recover; he just felt dead inside, knowing he would have to be strong for Roger, although at this precise second he just wanted to put a gun to his head and pull the trigger.

He couldn't imagine a life without Jackie and he certainly wasn't going to work for the agency any more, the price to pay was too high.

Roger was not quite 12 months old and he'd already lost his mother. James blamed himself for everything; if he hadn't met Jackie she would still be alive, he reasoned. Everything was his fault, no matter which way you looked at the situation.

Juliet catered to Roger's every need and supported James while he came to terms with the situation.

Jackie was cremated to ensure no virus she'd been infected with could escape. Her parents were notified and didn't attend the ceremony. They were disgusted she had become involved with James they didn't even want to see Roger their grandchild. James felt he should go and put a bullet between their eyes for being so cruel to their daughter.

A month had passed since the funeral. James had told Mary he could no longer work for her. She explained to him you just can't quit once you're a member of the agency, you are always a member. Juliet was ordered back to London by the end of the week and James would have to make arrangements for Roger's well-being. Once James had fully recovered he was required for new assignments.

James would watch television and occasionally play with Roger. Juliet realised the only way to snap James back into action was to send him on a mission. She knew if it was anything to do with a member of Khan's family he wouldn't hesitate at having the chance to get his own back although that is not a reason under which you should operate.

Juliet phoned Mary asking her to give James a reason to get back in the saddle before she left. Mary phoned James. "James, she said firmly continuing, "Mr Khan Senior has come into the country, we have agents monitoring him, we need him to disappear. He is part of the terrorist organisation and a threat to national security."

Juliet watched the smile come across James's face she could see the anger raging in his eyes in a whirlpool of hate. "I'll take the job, what are your instructions?"

"Firstly, wear your badge camera, I want to see what you're doing; you are to eliminate him and the guards he has with him and set fire to the premises to disguise what has taken place and leave no evidence you were there."

"My pleasure Mary," he replied coldly.

"James, be professional please."

Mary realised it was risky sending James on such a mission in his present state of mind. She was desperate to have him back in action; he would become a really good agent; it was just a pity he got off to such a bad start, losing his wife the way he did.

Mary knew there was an attraction between Juliet and James, although it was the agency's policy since she lost her husband in action, not to fraternise with other members to avoid decisions being made with the heart and not the mind, when under pressure.

Chapter 11
Out of Control

James set off after receiving a warning from Juliet to be careful, and she reminded him he had a son to come home to, and not to do anything stupid. He kissed her on the cheek which took her rather by surprise, she smiled in appreciation; this was the first time he had paid any attention to anyone since Jackie's death.

At 11 o'clock in the evening he arrived in Warwick, and checked his firearm was loaded and his knife was strapped to his leg. He could see a guard outside walking around the premises. James worked his way through the undergrowth as quietly as he could. Removing his knife, he came up behind the guard and slit his throat. The guard dropped like a stone. James then deactivated the alarm, something he was familiar with. He attached the silencer to his gun. Making his way to the front door he eased it open after picking the locks.

Going into the living room where he found a guard watching television quietly, he immediately put two bullets in his head and headed upstairs, finding another guard sitting on a chair almost asleep. He put one bullet in his head; the only sound was a slight thud as the gun fired.

James opened the bedroom door to find Mr Khan Senior in bed with his wife. James turned the light on, shooting Mrs Khan in the head. Mr Khan jumped out of bed. James shot him in each kneecap; he rolled on the floor in agony. James reloaded his gun, shooting Mr Khan in each shoulder, then removed his knife, stabbing him through the heart, and then drawing his knife all the way down his chest, opening him up like a gutted fish.

Not Guilty

Mary had been watching everything and was horrified with the way James had dealt with Mr Khan. She knew he would want revenge, but she didn't realise how angry James had become, and cold-blooded.

James, in no hurry, searched through the drawers beside the bed finding a wad of money which he put in his pocket. Mary heard him say, "That seemed a fair price for my services." He ran downstairs removing the guard he'd left in the garden and bringing him into the house.

James loosened the nut on the gas pipe, running upstairs and lighting a candle by Mr Khan's bed. He then left the premises.

Mary spoke to him. "What do you think you're doing James you're out of control you're starting to worry me."

"I dealt with the situation. I did exactly what you asked."

"Torturing him was not necessary, a simple shot to the head would have been sufficient." James didn't respond.

Mary remembered what she'd done to the person who had killed her husband; she had peeled the agent like a banana until he became unconscious with the pain and then put a bullet in his head, so in reality she was no different to him and the way he feels.

James returned home feeling a lot more settled. Juliet was waiting for him, some of her mannerisms reminded him so much of Jackie they could have almost been sisters. Juliet commented "Mary phoned me and told me what you did. You shouldn't have done that James, I know you want revenge and you're angry but nothing will bring Jackie back." James didn't respond.

James commented. "I wish you weren't returning to London, I will miss you and so will Roger."

"Mary has ordered me to stay for another week, I think you frightened the hell out of her and that would take some doing."

James smiled placing his hand either side of Juliet's face and kissing her on the lips. "That's good news," he continued, "I do enjoy having you around, you're a lovely person and very kind, especially to Roger."

"James you're being unfair to me and yourself, we both know how we feel about each other. In our line of business, it's stupid to become involved with each other as much as I want to." Juliet remarked sitting on the settee holding her coffee in both hands staring into the liquid for a solution to her feelings.

"I must confess," he said sitting by her, continuing. "I feel as guilty as hell I just can't get you out of my mind and Jackie hasn't been dead two months."

"I think the sooner I returned to London the better for everyone's sake. I just wish I could take Roger with me I love him so much."

James scratched his head and held his face in his hands. "Oh God," he said looking to the ceiling. "What the hell shall I do when you're gone?"

"Don't talk like that James, it's just as hard for me. I'm going to pack my bags, I'm leaving at daybreak. I can't stay here any longer."

Mary phoned at 3 o'clock in the morning, which was unusual for her. She told Juliet to switch her phone on speaker so James could hear. "Hi Mary what's up?" James asked.

"You're not going to like this much James; we don't have any choice. I need Juliet to impersonate Jackie and play the part as your wife."

"You can't be bloody serious, Mary," Juliet protested.

"That's not all, I want you both to fly to Malta, taking Roger as well, making believe you are just on holiday as a family."

"Why Mary it must be very important if you're considering risking my son Roger, and I haven't agreed yet," he said firmly.

"No, Mary you can't involve Roger, he is only a baby, I will go over your head, I refuse to use Roger as a decoy in any operation," Juliet responded firmly.

"Calm down Juliet, your feelings are getting the better of you girl, let me finish. You two and Roger will pose as tourists. There are a group of terrorists hiding in St Paul's Bay in a flat. They are part of Khan's organisation," Mary said, knowing full well the moment she mentioned Khan's name, nothing on this earth would stop James from killing them.

"How many, Mary?" James asked, with eagerness in his voice.

"Four in total at present, we need you to assassinate them and have their bodies removed from the flat, into one of our vehicles, and we will clean up the mess."

"And where is Roger while this is going on, who's going to look after him?" Juliet snapped.

"Me, I will be in Malta to at our headquarters he will stay with me while you to deal with the problem," she pointed out, continuing, "I've already booked you three a flight for Monday morning, Birmingham airport at 8 o'clock take off, the tickets will be waiting for you there. Juliet, use Jackie's passport, leave your weapons behind, you'll be re-equipped when you arrive."

"How did you know I'd agree Mary?" James asked suspiciously.

"I know how you feel about Khan and his organisation. I wasn't born yesterday, James," she said frostily.

Juliet complained: "James, you can't risk Roger for any reason, you're being stupid."

"Shut up Juliet," Mary instructed," and do as you are told my patience is wearing thin with you, girl."

Juliet exhaled, "Okay, if anything happens to Roger you will answer to me Mary."

"I understand Juliet. Roger will be in no danger at all, you have my word on that. He is only being used to create an illusion of a happily married family." Mary rang off.

"You can't threaten Mary, Juliet, don't be so stupid," James said, placing his arms around Juliet's shoulder. She lent her head against his. "I will kill her if anything happens to Roger and she knows I mean it," she said calmly.

"You're making your feelings pretty obvious Juliet."

"I know, I just can't help myself when it concerns Roger and you."

James retired to bed and Juliet lay on the top as she always did. James found it difficult at times to sleep when Juliet was snoring, although it made him smile. He awoke the next morning to find Juliet had moved. He could hear her in the front room telling Roger how much she loved him as she playing with him; he was becoming quite a handful.

James heard him call Juliet mommy, he watched through the crack of the door Juliet kissing him on the forehead and telling him how much she loved him. James didn't know what the hell to do. He wanted to be with Juliet and he knew Roger wanted her more than him. He couldn't imagine the situation ending happily. Sooner or later Juliet and he would have to part and go on separate missions.

Monday morning 6 am, Juliet prepared Roger for travelling and James packed his suitcase. They used Juliet's car to go to the airport and left it in the car park. Juliet presented Jackie's passport at customs and it was accepted without question. The flight took 3 ½ hours and after clearing customs, a car was already waiting for them. Juliet drove the hire car to a secluded property by the blue lagoon in the countryside.

Mary contacted them, advising where their weapons were to be found in the building. She told them that they were to stay there until they received further instructions and just to behave like normal tourists.

Juliet wore her bikini which did nothing to improve James's blood pressure, she had an outstanding figure. Juliet commented. "Stop staring at my body, we are supposed to be married, so you should have seen it all before."

James laughed. "I wish I could have remembered the honeymoon I must have been absolutely blotto."

James who was sitting in the other deckchair close to her received a slap on the belly. Roger was standing sucking on Juliet's leg. "You lucky boy, I'm not allowed to do that." Roger laughed as if he understood what his dad had said, Juliet just grinned.

The following morning, they were summoned to the office. Mary was waiting for them; she took Roger from Juliet's arms. He grizzled for a moment then obviously remembered he liked playing with Mary's glasses which annoyed her intensely.

"Tonight's the night, there are still only four in the flat. Here's the address." She passed a piece of paper to Juliet.

James commented: "There is no need to involve Juliet, I can deal with these people myself."

"You probably could James, we must make sure you are quick and clean, we do not want to disturb the neighbours, so make sure you fit your silencers. A cleaning team will be waiting. They will clear up after you have gone."

"Perhaps I should deal with this situation, I've more experience than James," Juliet remarked, blushing slightly."

"Oh please, when will you two get a room! You know my policy on becoming involved with other agents."

James didn't comment; he could feel his face burning with embarrassment. They left Roger with Mary and went outside. James reached for Juliet's hand and she didn't resist. They walked along the shoreline hand-in-hand, neither of them knowing what to do to control the situation. Juliet took the initiative: "Perhaps we should sleep together. I know I want to and I guess you do," she concluded.

James didn't respond. He released her hand, placing his arm around her waist until they reached the car. Juliet drove them back to their rented accommodation.

"You didn't answer my question, James," she said quietly.

"I thought of nothing else for months from the first time I met you," he confessed.

Juliet turned to face him surprised by his comment, she was convinced he was madly in love with Jackie still. "I didn't realise you'd felt that way for so long."

"I can't take you to bed Juliet, I don't want a one night stand I want you in my life forever."

His comment took Juliet by surprise; she was not prepared or even knew how to respond, whether she should feel insulted or overjoyed.

Juliet embraced him. James responded likewise: "I'm in love with you Juliet, I don't mind if I'm killed but I couldn't face the loss of another person I love being killed."

Chapter 12
Finding a Solution

They waited till midnight before attempting to enter the flat where the terrorists were situated. Juliet tried the door handle quietly, the door was not locked. They burst in switching on the light only to find the four terrorists asleep. Juliet shot the two on the right and James took the two on the left. Just as they were about to leave they could hear somebody whimpering; they knew it couldn't be the terrorists because they'd been shot in the head.

James opened a cupboard and found a woman tied up. Juliet quickly phoned Mary and appraised her of the situation. Mary instructed them both to leave the woman where she was and she would deal with the situation, they were to return to the office and collect Roger and return to their holiday home without further delay.

When they arrived, Roger was fast asleep on the couch. Mary was trying to clean her glasses after giving Roger a sticky sweet with which he kindly layered her glasses. "Well done you two, another clean assignment; don't worry about the woman, we will release her once we find out who she is and what she was doing there."

"That son of yours James, has been driving me mad, he has more energy than I can handle," Mary smiled, continuing: "He even said hello to the Prime Minister after grabbing the phone, which I had to apologise for."

"I want to marry James, Mary, and I won't take no for an answer." James stared at Juliet then glanced to see the expression on Mary's face.

"I'm not surprised; you realise the pitfalls of being married to an operative which I found out to my own cost. I lost the love of my life," she commented.

"Do you feel the same way James? You obviously do by the expression on your face, please close your mouth," she smiled.

Juliet glanced to James who was still trying to come to terms with what Juliet had said; it was something he really wanted but didn't quite expect Juliet to be storming in like a bull in a china shop to get her own way, especially against Mary.

Mary thought for a moment. "At least if you were married, no one would question you when you travel together, the added advantage of having two operatives together could be beneficial in some circumstances. Let me think on the matter overnight and I'll give you my answer tomorrow now take Roger home and get some well-deserved rest the pair of you," she instructed.

James carefully lifted Roger from the couch; trying not to wake him, they made their way back to their accommodation, placing Roger in his cot.

Juliet made them both a drink. "You do want to marry me James don't you?"

James got down on one knee and held her hand. "Will you marry me please?"

Juliet's smile broadened she had never felt so happy for as long as she could remember she'd had the casual boyfriend who only ever wanted to take her to bed. That wasn't what she was looking for in a man so they didn't get very far with her.

James commented "We can buy our rings over here while were on holiday," He suggested.

"We've still have to wait for Mary's answer hopefully she will give in but you can't really tell with her," Juliet commented kissing James on the lips.

James retired to bed; Juliet followed, instead of sleeping on the top of the bed as she always had done. This time she slid under the sheets, he felt her warm body against his. She placed her arm across his chest hoping for a response.

James turned his back to her which she thought was rather insulting or perhaps he just didn't realise she was in bed with him. She pressed her breasts against the middle of his back and slid her hand down his thigh.

James was fully awake trying not to laugh he knew exactly what Juliet was doing. She lay on her back frustrated after a few minutes receiving no response from him. James rolled back over onto his other side and gently started kissing Juliet's neck, arm then her lips, sliding down onto her breast, within a little while they were making love to each other with exhilarating passion.

After breakfast, Juliet dressed Roger, continually looking across and smiling to James who in turn smiled back. James had given Juliet something she longed for all her life; true love, someone who wanted her for what she was not just a sex toy.

James on the other hand was feeling rather guilty; in some respects feeling he had slightly betrayed Jackie's memory and the love he had for her.

They drove into Valetta, parking the car and James removing the collapsible pushchair from the boot. They strolled along holding each other, looking into all the jewellery shop windows. Juliet suddenly caught sight of a ring with a beautiful diamond that sparkled in the sunlight. They went inside; the ring was 2000 Euros. James paid for it immediately and the jeweller adjusted the ring to fit Juliet's finger. Her smile could have lit the darkest sky. James had never seen her look so happy and content in the short while he'd known her.

Juliet's mobile rang; Mary. "I see you purchased a ring already." Juliet looked around studying all the streets in her view she couldn't see Mary anywhere: "Where are you, Mary?"

Mary chuckled, "The coffee shop across the road. I've been watching you, young lady, come and join me."

James had overheard the conversation and looked across to see Mary sitting outside in the shade of a parasol. They walked across, sitting at the table with Mary. Mary held Juliet's hand looking at the ring commenting, "Lovely ring." Mary ordered coffee for everyone and a large ice cream for Roger, who protested at being left in the pushchair, until he received his ice cream, then all was silent.

"How did you know what my answer was going to be Juliet?" Mary asked trying to betray a stern expression.

"I didn't; we just hoped and tried to be positive, what is your answer?" Juliet enquired.

"I spoke to my superiors and after some lengthy consultation they have agreed it could be beneficial to the agency and also could be a disaster, if one of you is captured on a mission, I've been there and seen what it does to a person."

James asked cautiously "Mary, would you be a godparent to Roger, in case something happens to me?" He placed his hand on top of Mary's and squeezed gently. "Please, you're one of the few people I can trust and call a friend."

Mary stared at his expression then glanced down at his hand resting on hers, glancing back with tear filled eyes. "This is the second time you taken me by surprise, I would be honoured, yes."

Juliet smiled. Mary slid her hand from under his. "Stop flirting with your boss please," she muttered.

James happened to glance up to a window across the street, seeing the reflection of a telescopic sight on a rifle. He shouted, "Get down." He removed his gun from his jacket pocket, taking aim, shooting the gunman, watching him fall from the window into the stree,t clutching a sniper's rifle. James quickly put his gun in his pocket. People scattered in every direction. Roger was crying. Juliet scooped him up from the push-chair. Mary instructed everyone to scatter; in the confusion they would disappear. Juliet and James made their way back to the car and returned to their accommodation.

Mary made contact. "Are you safe?"

"Yes, Mary," James replied. "Are you okay? if not I'll come and get you"

Mary laughed. "I was a field agent once James, I know how to look after myself thank you all the same. You realise the gun was aimed at me. I would have been a great prize if the terrorist could have eliminated me. It was my fault I put you in danger by calling you across to me."

"Do we know who it was, Mary?" Juliet asked.

"No, we are talking to the police at the moment to extract as much information as we can. In the meantime, I need you two on a plane back to England. The tickets are waiting for you at the airport; you leave at 9 o'clock in the morning." She rang off.

James exhaled, "I wouldn't have minded a few more days here, just us three." Juliet smiled, "It doesn't matter where we are as long as were together, James."

James turned the television on only to see himself shooting the assassin, videoed by a bloody tourist. James stared in horror. Juliet placed her arm around his shoulder: "Damn we could have done without that exposure."

James's phone rang. "Have you seen the news?" Mary asked concerned.

"Yes, just."

"This is what I want you to do. Pack your things, drive to the docks and board HMS Princess, she's in port. Once you're on board you are on

British territory; she is due to leave in the next hour, so get your skates on, we will dispose of the car."

They quickly packed and drove to the docks, removing their belongings from the car and boarding the ship; they were hurriedly guided down below to a cabin. James looked out of a porthole to see their car being driven away. Just before they were to set sail, Mary boarded the ship herself and joined them below, very calmly picking up Roger in her arms. "And how's my Godchild, then?" she said.

Juliet and James sat and watched Mary playing with Roger as if there was nothing wrong. "By the way James, thanks you for saving my life, excellent marksmanship too at that distance with a handgun."

A sailor knocked on the door and entered. "Director, the captain has asked to see you in his quarters to ascertain your requirements."

"Tell him I will be there shortly; I'm playing with my godson." The sailor saluted, leaving, shutting the door behind him.

James and Juliet smiled at her response to a captain's request. Mary was in charge and she made sure everyone knew; she would not be pushed around by anyone unless it suited her.

Once they were at sea, they boarded a helicopter and were flown back to Birmingham airport. Mary stayed on board the helicopter, to fly on to London. Juliet and James returned home to the caravan park. Juliet fed and changed Roger and put him in his cot. James went out in his van to acquire some groceries in town.

Juliet heard a knock at the door. She looked out of the window to see a man and a woman standing there smartly dressed. She thought they might be Jehovah's Witnesses, nevertheless she wasn't taking any risks; she parted her coat, placing her hand on her gun, and opened the door. The gentleman spoke looking rather surprised by Juliet's stance displaying her badge and gun in the holster. "I believe James Thompson lives here; I'm his father," he said nervously, "and this is his mother." Juliet invited them in cautiously. They seated themselves on the settee looking very uncomfortable. "James is in trouble again I see your badge and gun," Mr Thompson asked, continuing: "We understand his wife died, and you are? May I ask?"

"I think I should make one or two things very clear," Juliet said firmly, continuing: "James is not guilty of attempted rape. She fabricated the evidence." Juliet watched his parents look at each other in shock. She continued: "I work for the government and so does James, my future husband."

Not Guilty

"We heard he had a son," Mrs Thompson asked. Juliet answered: "Roger is asleep. I'm here guarding him while James is away, he shouldn't be long, if you care to wait I will make you a drink."

Mr and Mrs Thompson looked at each other, holding hands. "James was never guilty?" Mrs Thompson asked. "No! Jennifer fabricated the story because James refused to hack into the school computers so she could copy the exam answers," answered Juliet.

Mrs Thompson burst into tears: "We should have believed him Gerald, he's never lied to us."

Juliet passed them a coffee and returned to the kitchen sink where she could watch them closely.

James returned carrying in a box of groceries; he stood and stared at them both for a moment then looked to Juliet and placed the groceries on the table.

His parents stood up together. "Were sorry, James, this young lady just told us the truth." James removed his jacket displaying his gun in his holster and his badge.

His parents stared. "You work for the government too?" James nodded. "We don't know how to make it up to you James, we should have believed your story, just all the evidence was stacked against you."

James finally responded. "Meet my future wife, Juliet."

They both shook her hand cautiously. James explained what had happened to Jackie without giving too many details away.

His parents conveyed their wish to be involved with Roger and to be a part of his life and his new wife to be. Roger was tired and James didn't want to disturb him, so he explained to his father and mother that they would bring him round the next afternoon. Mr and Mrs Thompson hugged James and Juliet before leaving after staying for a couple of hours.

James embraced Juliet and whispered in her ear, "I love you." Juliet held his hand and led him into the bedroom so they could rest after such a traumatic journey from Malta.

Chapter 13
Love Will Triumph

James and Juliet married at the local registry office a few weeks later. His parents offered to have Roger while they went on their honeymoon to Scotland. James and Juliet agreed for the two-week break they were taking, although they were never really off duty, they always had to carry their weapons with them in case of an emergency.

They drove the 500 miles to Nairn, and parked in the hotel car park. After registering with reception, they made their way to the honeymoon suite, where James scooped Juliet up in his arms and carried her over the threshold. After their evening meal, they walked along the shoreline gazing out over the sea, wondering what the future held for them. At this precise moment, all that mattered was that they were together and in love.

Juliet's mobile rang; she answered, "What you mean, Mary's gone missing?" she said, concerned. Juliet continued: "Yes Minister, thank you Minister, we will do what we can, we will find her."

"Who the hell were you talking to, and what's this about Mary?"

Juliet explained: "Mary has gone missing, her flat appears to have been broken into although it's high security; they have bypassed the alarm system somehow. No one knows where to look, we have no Intel, no one heard any chatter of an impending attempt on Mary's life.

James asked "Where do we start to look?"

"I don't know, James, they took her out of London for sure."

James sat on a bench looking out to the sea. "I don't think they will kill her straight away, they will want information from her first."

Juliet sat beside him for a moment; then they both returned to the hotel, packed their bags and made some excuse why they were leaving, having no idea where she could be in the country or in the world by now, for that matter.

James commented: "Some bloody honeymoon."

Juliet smiled, reached across and squeezed his hand. "We have to assist, James, it's Mary, she's been good to us both." They drove through the night, hoping and praying they would receive news of Mary's whereabouts. Stephen, a new operative, spoke over the intercom in the car. "James, a lorry has been stolen with a container on the back; we think Mary's inside, where are you now?"

"About 5 miles from the Sandbach slip road on the M6."

"I've been instructed to tell you to wait there just off the motorway and watch for a red and yellow lorry with a container on the back, with Emirates shipping stamped on the side."

James pulled off the motorway. Juliet was asleep in the passenger seat after driving the first stage of the journey home. Juliet stirred, James explained everything to her; they sat watching the traffic checking their firearms. An hour drifted past and no signs of anything. Juliet spotted a lorry leaving the motorway and heading for Sandbach, carrying the container with the correct logo they were searching for.

James drove, overtaking the lorry, which was travelling at a normal speed. James tore off down the road, gaining some distance, skidded to a halt and told Juliet to get out. She stared at him. "Do as you're bloody told. If I can't stop the lorry shoot the radiator, it will seize the engine." She jumped out, horrified at James's expression.

James placed his gun on the passenger seat and started reversing back up the road at high speed Juliet was horrified, seeing the headlights of her car fading; she saw the lorry headlights coming into view and sparks flying everywhere. She heard gunfire; she positioned herself behind a bus stop ready to shoot.

James had shot through the back window of the car piercing the radiator, holding his foot brake down as hard as he could. The lorry continued to push the car with little effort. Juliet could see machine-gun fire and feared for James's life.

Suddenly the lorry swerved, twisting the car sideways, and it started to roll like a barrel down the road, bursting into flames. Juliet shot the driver dead and the lorry stopped. She shot the passenger. She ran to the back of the container opening the door and shot Mary's captor dead. Juliet climbed into the back of the container, releasing Mary who was battered and bruised but otherwise unharmed.

Juliet helped Mary out of the container; they both looked back up the road, to see the remains of Juliet's car mangled on the side of the road. They ran towards it as quick as they could, both knowing no one could survive in the wreckage.

They both searched, James wasn't there; a little way further up the road, he lay on the grass unconscious. Mary took Juliet's mobile and made a call. Juliet knelt down beside James, crying; she checked for a pulse, looking to Mary: "He's alive." Mary had already phoned for an air ambulance, the police closed the road and James was airlifted directly to London, along with Juliet and Mary.

Mary held Juliet's hand. "Now do you understand what I meant about having a loved one in the service?"

Juliet nodded, "I don't care, I love him. I want to be with him all the time. Please don't die James, don't leave me."

Mary herself had experienced the same anguish with her husband and wished she could take the pain away from Juliet. "You have a brave man there, to take on a lorry with a car. I must discipline him when he's recovered."

The medic informed Mary that James had a broken arm and a broken leg, he couldn't tell if there were any internal injuries until James was x-rayed.

After landing, James was checked out and placed in bed. Mary had been slapped a few times and she had a swollen eye where she'd been punched and was given the all clear by the doctors. They went to see James, who was now conscious and in plaster.

He looked immediately to Juliet and smiled. Mary shook her head and bent down and kissed him on the forehead. "You're a brave fool James and you owe the agency a car." She smiled, continuing: "Thank you for saving my life once again."

James commented, "You will have to come on honeymoon with us at, least I'll know where you are," he joked.

Mary smiled. Turning to the doctor, she asked: "When can he leave?"

"We'd like to keep him overnight, he can go in the morning; he is only bruised apart from his broken arm and leg."

Mary placed her arm around Juliet. "They are holding the honeymoon suite for you to in Nairn," Mary said. "The owner is an old friend of mine.

A new car for you, Juliet, will be delivered there. I will arrange for a helicopter to take you both back to the hotel in the morning."

Juliet kissed Mary on the cheek. "Thank you, thank you for everything."

Mary smiled and left the room. Juliet seated herself beside James; "I thought I'd lost you when I saw the state of the car."

James commented, "Would you like to slide into bed, my wife, I'm sure I could manage," h e joked.

Juliet blushed. "No, not here, rest and wait till tomorrow."

There was a knock on the door which opened; standing in the doorway was a messenger.

He passed the sealed envelope to Juliet saying, "Her Majesty the Queen has instructed me to deliver this message to you, Mr James Thompson." He turned and left immediately.

James joked. "Probably a bloody bill for the car I wrecked."

Juliet examined the envelope. "Queen's Seal shall I open it for you?"

James nodded.

Juliet broke the seal removing the letter on her Majesty's personal paper.

"James," Juliet gasped. "The Queen expresses her gratitude for your bravery saving Mary's life"

"That's unfair," James commented. "You played a bigger part than me."

"I don't think so James, I wasn't the one rolling along inside a burning car I'm not the one with a broken arm and leg. You could have been killed."

James flipped the bed sheets over to one side. "I want my reward now I'm a hero," he laughed.

Juliet grinned. "Stop it James, I'll see you in the morning." She kissed him on the forehead and left the room.

James was drifting off to sleep when he heard the door open quietly, he could see someone approaching through the dim light. He guessed the nurse was not what she seemed, approaching the bed very stealthily. He didn't move and pretended to be asleep, watching out of the corner of his eye. She removed a large knife from inside her uniform.

James grabbed her hand, rolling out of bed on top of her. She was shouting in Arabic at him; he was struggling one-handed to control her with the knife. The door burst open and a soldier placed his gun to her head and spoke to her in Arabic.

Doctors rushed in, helping James back into bed and checking his plasters hadn't been compromised in the struggle.

Mary came in horrified, shouting: "Who's in charge of security, I want their head." She moved across to James, pushing the doctor out of the way. James had never seen Mary look so angry. "I can only apologise James I will investigate I promise you somebody will answer for what's happened," she said, storming out of the room. A little while later Juliet came running in.

"You missed all the fun my love," he smiled.

"Mary phoned, explained what happened and told Juliet to stay with James till she finds out what's going on."

James smiled throwing the covers open on his bed. "Climb aboard my love."

"Oh, very well," She removed her coat and shoes and slid beneath the sheets alongside James with her gun on top of the sheet.

"I knew I would get my own way eventually," James smiled.

"Move your hand away James, or I'll put a bullet in your foot," she smiled.

Being attacked nearly every day of the week no longer bothered James, it just seemed normal to him. Juliet was puzzled why he always made light of a potentially fatal situation. She was determined she was not going to lose her husband through not being vigilant.

Mary came back into the room shaking her head and smiling: "I told you to guard him Juliet not smother him."

Mary sat on the chair beside the bed. "The woman who attacked you, James, was a member of a terrorist cell. You killed her husband in Malta and she was seeking revenge. Thank God she wasn't wearing explosives we'd been picking you off the ceiling." Mary exhaled and continued: "I have replaced the head of security here; hopefully that will be the end to any more incidents."

She headed for the door, glancing back. "James, don't distract Juliet, she is here to protect you while you're incapacitated. A helicopter is booked for the morning." Mary left the room, closing the door quietly behind her.

Juliet kissed James passionately on the lips. "Mary's right, don't distract me James, move your hand please."

"Okay spoilsport."

"James I need to go to the loo. Here's my gun while I'm gone."

Juliet opened the door to see two soldiers one either side of the door. Mary was taking no chances over James's security.

Chapter 14

Try Again

James was wheeled to the heliport on the roof of the hospital and helped into the helicopter. Juliet joined him. They flew direct to the hotel, landing on the roof, which was reserved for VIP customers. The hotel staff assisted James to the honeymoon suite. A large bowl of fruit had been placed in the room along with a bottle of champagne in an ice bucket and two glasses. The hotel manager greeted them both and wished them a pleasant stay in his establishment and if they wanted anything, just to phone.

Juliet looked out of the bedroom window to see a brand-new BMW parked outside, with a new child seat fitted in the back. Juliet locked the door after putting a do not disturb sign on the outside. She helped James undress, remarking, "We will have to go shopping later on or in the morning; all our clothes were burned when you trashed my car," she smiled.

Juliet removed her clothes, placing her gun on the bedside table and slid into bed beside James. They were soon making love with Juliet on top of him. A little while later Juliet showered, returning to help James to the bathroom to wash himself down. He couldn't shower while wearing plaster casts.

James in a wheelchair and Juliet pushing him, they made their way to the lift and down to the ground floor of the hotel, continuing into the town, to shop for new clothes for both of them. James's wheelchair was loaded down with all the purchases. A member of the hotel staff was passing and offered to take their purchases to the hotel on their behalf which was greatly appreciated by them both. James phoned his parents to see how Roger was behaving.

His mother answered, "He's wonderful James we are so proud of you, how's your honeymoon going we both hope you're enjoying yourself son?"

Juliet snatched the phone from James's hand. "He's not much use I'm afraid with a broken arm and leg, that will teach him to jump off the wardrobe." Juliet joked.

"Don't panic mother." James said, retrieving his phone, smiling at Juliet's comment. "I fell down the stairs leading onto the beach, nothing to worry about."

"Oh, dear James please be careful and don't drink too much."

"No mother, I'll phone you again soon, bye."

"You make a good slave Juliet my love." She smacked him around the ear, leaving him in the wheelchair and walked on ahead. "Hey, I was only joking," he said.

Juliet started walking towards him: "I don't think your mother likes me James."

"Tough, although I can understand her point of view, considering it was a shotgun wedding; you forced me to get married, you wicked woman, just so you could have your way with me."

"Don't get too comfortable, when you're out of this chair you can wait on me."

They returned to the hotel, James lying on the bed. Their new purchases were in the room waiting for them to unpack.

James phoned down to reception, requesting a romantic meal for two in their room; at least he thought if they were in here, the chances of being shot or molested were very slim. Juliet changed into a dress, looking at herself in the mirror, brushing her long black hair.

Later on, there was a knock at the door and in walked a waiter, carrying a table, and with him two maids setting it out, with all the trimmings, including a chilled bottle of champagne. James hobbled his way to the table. "Good evening your ladyship, my name is James. James Bond, you can call me 007."

He poured the champagne into the awaiting glasses; Juliet was screaming with laughter: "You fool James."

He'd also ordered red roses and a necklace inscribed "I will always love you, James," when Juliet was having a shower; a piece of jewellery he'd seen in the shop window while they were out.

Not Guilty

James waited for the knock on the door before their meal was served. Knock, knock. The door opened and in walked the head waiter, carrying the bouquet of red roses and a small velvet box tied with a pink bow. The waiter carefully placed them on the table, in front of Juliet. She placed her hands to her mouth in astonishment and surprise. The waiter left.

"James, oh James." She noticed the little box and opened it, revealing a gold chain with a heart-shaped locket she looked inside and saw the inscription. She rose to her feet quickly and kissed James passionately "I will always love you too James." Tears ran down her cheeks. "Oh God I'm glad I have you. You make me feel complete."

The waiter returned a few minutes later, lighting the candles on the table, taking the flowers from Juliet and placing them in a vase; he then stood by the door and snapped his fingers; more waiters appeared carrying their first course and left. James passed the head waiter a £50 note saying, "Thank you, spot on."

After they'd finished their three course meal, they sat quietly sipping champagne. Juliet went to the mirror, fitting her new gift around her neck and admiring it. James was becoming frustrated with the plaster on his leg and arm, they impeded him a great deal. He wondered if he dare try walking, which he did, much to Juliet's annoyance. "Come on Juliet, let's go for walk, I'll be careful." She placed a sock over his bare toes to stop them getting cold. "Thanks mom," James joked.

"You ever do as you're told James?"

"Very rarely," he remarked, attaching his gun to his belt and checking it was loaded, slid his coat over his left shoulder to cover his holster from view. Juliet slid hers into her handbag, now she was wearing a dress she had nowhere else to put it.

"You know what James? I've just realised you're left-handed."

James smiled, "That's my cuddling arm," placing it around her waist and kissing her gently on the lips.

"Come on, if you insist on going for a walk, but only a short one James, I don't want you back in hospital."

They made their way outside. Juliet supporting him, they walked across to have a look at Juliet's new car. She pressed the fob and the car burst into flames. They moved away as quickly as they could. The fire brigade was there in seconds, as they were only just down the road.

Juliet phoned Mary and told what had happened. Mary was silent for a moment. "First we have to establish whether it's a fault with the car, or whether it had been tampered with. As long as you are both okay. I will have a new car for you in the morning," she commented with concern, continuing, "I think you will have to end your honeymoon early and come home, someone from the agency has information on your whereabouts, we must have another mole." Mary rang off.

Juliet suggested they went back inside. James remarked, "No, I want to go for a walk and I bloody well will, no bloody terrorist is going to stop me," he said, becoming angry at the thought. Juliet could have been in the car when it caught fire, along with Roger.

Juliet saw his frustration and rubbed his shoulder and kissed him on the neck which made him smile. They walked along the shoreline on the footpath, sitting on a bench, watching the ships in the distance.

James commented, "It's the government's fault, letting all these immigrants in, most of them are bloody terrorists I suspect."

Juliet cuddled up to him; the sea-breeze was turning cool. "Let's go back to the hotel James I'm getting cold, I'm not used to wearing a dress."

James remarked. "I thought you were a transvestite when I first met you with your hairy legs."

Juliet hit him so hard he rolled down the embankment, she put her hand to her mouth not realising she'd hit him so hard.

James was curled up with laughter. "I don't have hairy legs; I've never had hairy legs, you pig," she smiled, continuing, "If you're always going to be this cruel to me James…." Juliet dropped to the floor as if she'd been shot.

James removed his gun immediately and scrambled up the embankment to where Juliet was lying on the grass. He hadn't heard a shot although if they were using a silencer he wouldn't have. He couldn't see any blood. Juliet started to laugh. "I knew you love me, that'll teach you to insult me, you thought I'd been shot, didn't you?"

Juliet watched the tears forming in James's eyes, she hadn't realised how much she'd upset him; she was convinced he was built of stone. She went on her knees and held him. "I'm sorry, that was a silly trick to play."

"You do that again to me Juliet and I'll shoot you my bloody self," he remarked, wiping his eyes and smacking her backside.

They made their way back into the hotel and stayed in their room for the rest of the evening. Juliet was still concerned James thought she had hairy legs, so she lay naked beside him on the bed. "Check my legs, they're smooth."

"I'll do more than that," he said rolling onto her.

The next morning, they packed their bags and waited patiently in reception for the new car. Juliet's phone rang: "Hi, Mary," she said. Mary explained that there had been a device fitted to her car, causing it to burst into flames. They didn't know where it was fitted or when.

All new vehicles they used would now be fitted with a device that runs a security check looking for foreign objects, if one was found the office would be notified immediately to avoid a repetition of what happened the day before.

Juliet's new BMW arrived; they loaded their luggage into the boot and started for home.

James smiled: "I wonder how many other people have honeymoons like ours."

Mary came over the intercom: "How do you like your new car Juliet?"

"Fine Mary, thank you."

"Haven't you noticed?"

"Noticed what?"

"This one is fitted with bullet-proof glass, puncture resistant tyres; there is a handgun under each seat at the front, and a machine-gun in the boot, just press the red button on the seat and it will appear."

"We don't like the colour black, Mary," James commented.

"That's a shame James, they only come in that colour," not seeing the funny side of his comment, if he only knew the car cost £250,000 to build with all the extras.

"I think you've upset Mary, James." Juliet commented.

"I know she loves me really; she knew I was only joking."

"I'm still listening. I'll speak to you when you're home and in a more appreciative frame of mind."

They returned home at 7 o'clock in the evening and decided to leave Roger with James's parents for one more night. James carried the suitcases i;, realising his van was missing, he phoned Mary. "What's happened to my van, Mary? I hope it hasn't been stolen"

"No, we're having it modified slightly like the other vehicles to detect foreign objects being attached, you will have it back tomorrow, don't worry," she said firmly.

"Hey Mary, I owe you an apology, I didn't mean to be sarcastic and I realise you didn't see the funny side."

"I don't think you appreciate how hard my job is. I'm responsible for your welfare along with every other member of my team. Trying to outthink criminals is hard enough, without my agents cribbing about the colour of a car. Considering it cost the agency £250,000 to make and the reason the bulletproof glass was fitted was to protect my godson, not you or Juliet, and I paid for that myself."

James was silent. He didn't know how to respond, other than to say "Thank you, Mary." She ended the call.

James went inside and conveyed the conversation to Juliet who was making a coffee with some powdered milk she'd found in the cupboard. She turned to face James, "Oh my God that must have cost her a fortune."

They both retired to bed and drifted off to sleep peacefully, tired from their long journey. Early the next morning James was making breakfast and phoned his parents, they would be along shortly to collect Roger, they'd had to end the honeymoon earlier due to work issues.

Juliet was sick, she thought she had eaten a dodgy sandwich on the way home. They drove the short distance to James's parents, where Roger immediately clung to Juliet. James's father hugged Juliet and so did his mother.

They stayed there for a little while talking and then returned home. Juliet went to bed. She wasn't feeling well at all. James's van had been returned; they'd also repaired the bullet hole in the back door from his last encounter with terrorists.

James phoned Mary and reported Juliet was ill and he was concerned, although Juliet said she didn't want to see a doctor. Mary said, "Sod what she wants, I'm sending one now it could be more than food poisoning, after recent events we can take anything for granted, you were wise to report it to me." She rang off.

Half an hour later a doctor arrived and entered the static home. "Here's my card, ring Mary for confirmation."

Mary confirmed he was the doctor she sent. Juliet sat up in bed furious: "It's just food poisoning James, you're being stupid."

The doctor sat on the edge of the bed. "I'll be the judge of that Juliet. Mary sent me, and James is right to be concerned, he's being responsible, not like you, stupid."

Juliet sighed: "Sorry James, I just feel crap.

Not Guilty

The doctor took her temperature blood pressure and asked for a urine sample, which she provided. The doctor smiled, "You are in perfect health for someone who's pregnant."

"Rubbish," Juliet said. "I'm on the pill, oh, I did miss a few days when we were in Malta and on honeymoon."

"Don't take any more, it is too late now," the doctor instructed continuing: "I will leave you to explain the situation to Mary." He smiled and left.

James came into the bedroom, sitting beside her on the bed; she hugged him and started to cry. "What's wrong, Juliet?"

"I'm pregnant, Mary is going to kill me."

"Fabulous Roger is going to have a brother or sister." James kissed her on the forehead, over the moon with the news.

"Mary may make me have an abortion," she said, continuing to cry.

"Don't you want our child, Juliet?" James asked, concerned.

"Of course I do," she sobbed. "I can't be an agent and pregnant, the agency won't allow it."

"I'll talk to Mary," James said calmly: "Don't upset yourself, we'll work things out."

Chapter 15
Things Must Change

Mary phoned Juliet hearing Juliet crying. Mary said calmly: "You're pregnant. I guessed as much, we will have to find you a desk job. Don't worry Juliet, after all I did tell you two to get a room."

"Thank you for being so understanding, I'm terribly sorry. Would you like to be godmother to my child?"

"I would be honoured, Juliet, thank you."

James had overheard the conversation and took the phone from Juliet: "Thank you, Mary, you're a wonderful person and I love you for being understanding."

"You realise James, you will have to move to more secure location, you can stay in the area, but you must be protected by bricks and mortar I'm afraid; with adequate security protection, something we can monitor from here at headquarters."

"Anything you say Mary."

"First thing tomorrow James you and Juliet find a property you like and let me know."

"Will do."

"Congratulations to you both." Mary rang off.

After breakfast they went house hunting in Welford upon Avon, not far from their present home; they found a large bungalow on the outskirts of the village; the bungalow was surrounded by a hedge with a small adequate garden at the rear.

Juliet was really excited about the property. James phoned Mary, telling her where the property was and its situation. She replied "Give me a

Not Guilty

moment." She checked the property out from her office using satellite. She commented: "It is very suitable."

James said he was going to purchase it and Mary said she would have an electric fence fitted on the inside of the hedge and gates.

James phoned the agent who confirmed the property was still for sale for the sum of £250,000. James asked him if he could come straight out to give them access. The agent was there within 20 minutes.

The agent showed James and Juliet around the property, which was four bedroomed, a beautiful kitchen and a large lounge. James pulled a wad of cash from his pocket, counted out £250,000 and the agent gave him a receipt. The property agent was taken by surprise to see such a large sum of money in cash. He left them with the keys and assured them the paperwork would follow immediately giving them ownership.

Juliet asked. "Where did you get all that money from James?"

"Working for the agency, before I knew it was an agency."

Juliet frowned then smiled. "I don't know what you mean and I don't really care."

Juliet was really excited. She went around each room telling James what colour she wanted and what furniture. Roger was just laughing and he seemed to be excited as well.

James phoned the decorating firm to meet them at the property at 9 o'clock in the morning. They then left and drove on to a large furniture store. James held Roger in his arms saying to Juliet, "Buy what you want." Juliet was really happy, she spent £30,000 on furnishings and placed her hand to her mouth when her purchases were calculated on the till, she looked to James in shock. "Can we afford all this James?" James smiled, passing Roger to Juliet while he paid in cash again. They left the store after arranging delivery for early the next week.

"I have some money saved James, let me pay for something please."

"How much money have you saved?"

"I have about a hundred thousand pounds, plus my flat is worth another 200,000 at least."

"What happens if I'm killed Juliet, who will provide for the children?"

"Cheer me up, husband, you're turning me into a widow already"

"You have to think of these things unfortunately Juliet, God forbid it happens"

The next morning Juliet, Roger and James arrived at the new premises, only to find contractors everywhere and Mary with her clipboard ticking off jobs. "What's going on Mary?" James asked rather concerned he hadn't been consulted on anything, and he did own the house after all.

Mary smiled: "Good morning James. A perimeter fence is being fitted against the hedge 3 metres high; new gates electronically operated, external window blinds made from bullet-proof material which we can automatically close from head office should an intruder approach. The fourth bedroom we will turn into an office for Juliet to work out of. There will be external and internal security cameras." She held out her hand, showing James and Juliet a camera and listening device no larger than a 10p piece. "Oh I forgot to mention, at the rear of the house we'll fit a generator that will automatically start should there be a power cut," she smiled.

James glanced to Juliet commenting "I didn't think we were that important to splash out this sort of cash."

"You're not James," Mary said firmly. "The equipment going into your property is, and of course so is Roger," she said, tickling him under the chin. "Yes, Juliet, and before you ask you can choose the colours in the bungalow and I know you've already purchased the furniture."

Juliet grumbled, "Is there nothing we can do without you knowing Mary?"

Mary chuckled placing her hand on Juliet's stomach, "Obviously."

Mary removed her glasses, placing them in her coat pocket and taking Roger from Juliet. One or two of the neighbours walked past slowly trying to see what was going on, with so many people working on the property. The decorator arrived; Juliet took great pleasure in instructing what paper she wanted on the walls and paint colours. James placed his arm around Mary. "You're an old softy on the quiet Mary," he kissed her on the cheek.

Mary blushed and didn't respond. James was desperate to get rid of the plaster casts on his arm and leg, there's nothing worse than having an itch you can't scratch. After half an hour, Juliet returned to Mary and James. "James it will cost £9000 to decorate; I'll cover the cost." Mary commented. "You will certainly not young lady," Mary said, passing the decorator her card. She warned: "Make sure you do an excellent job, otherwise you will have me after you and that's something you will not forget," Mary smiled. "I'm taking my godson to the park in Stratford to spoil him," she said with authority.

"What about security, Director?"

"Finally you realise I'm your boss," she smiled.

They followed Mary out onto the road, seeing a brand-new Jaguar parked across the entrance, with a driver and another agent in the front. The driver got out; James noted he was fully armed as his coat parted opening the rear door for Mary and Roger to slide in; she'd even had a car seat fitted. James placed his arm around Juliet's waist, they both felt comfortable with Mary taking Roger with two armed agents. Mary lowered the window "You're not the only one who can have a new car," she joked, which seemed out of character for Mary, although Roger seemed to bring in her.

Juliet and James could not understand why they were being treated so specially, and how Mary had managed to acquire funding to alter a house that didn't belong to the agency. They both agreed there was something going on they weren't being told about. They both knew it would be futile trying to extract information from Mary, you might as well talk to a brick wall. You get just as much information.

Juliet put her hand to her mouth. "Damn, I forgot about carpets in all the excitement. I'm becoming a right dum dum."

They heard Mary's voice "Already taken care of."

James spoke up, "What's going on Mary? You seem to know our every movement and our every thought."

There was no reply, they continued the short distance home. Juliet commented as they went inside: "I feel like a lab rat, James, involved in an experiment I don't understand."

James nodded in agreement and went out to the van, unlocking and removing a device for detecting bugs. He entered the static, placing his finger to his lips. Juliet didn't speak. She knew what he was doing. As he suspected, his property was bugged; Mary could hear every word they were saying, which he thought was rather underhanded, considering they were members of the same organisation and supposed to be working as a team.

Juliet went into their bedroom, James followed and checked the room for bugs. He couldn't detect any. Juliet started to change her top. James grabbed her from behind, placing his hands on her firm breasts and kissing her neck tenderly. She released her bra and removed her jeans, lying on the bed waiting for him.

Three hours later Mary returned with Roger. James was determined to ascertain what was going on and why his static home was bugged. Mary dismissed his complaint as standard practice for all agency staff, including herself. She stayed for a coffee and then left, kissing Roger on the forehead before leaving.

Chapter 16

Moving House

A week had passed. James had been in touch with an agent, placing his static home up for sale, lock stock and barrel. They weren't taking anything with them. Juliet had purchased everything brand-new for the bungalow right down to the last plate.

Juliet watched in amazement, as James went into the cupboard, removing two tiles and pulling out a wad of cash and stuffing it in his pocket. She commented, "How many more secrets?"

James removed the money from his pocket: "Here, you can have it if you want, it's from work I carried out before I became an agent."

"What did you do James?"

"Do you really want me to tell you? I would sooner forget personally?"

"Mary obviously knew what you were doing, otherwise she'd have stopped you."

"Apparently so, and I thought I was clever."

"You might as well tell me James, what did you do?"

"Kill people," he said sitting down on the settee holding his head. "I was angry with the world and what had happened to me. I became judge and executioner, after assessing the situation."

"Oh," Juliet flopped down beside him. "I didn't expect you to say that, James." She then smiled: "That's the past, let's look forward to our future together and our child to be."

They each drove their own vehicle, heading for the new property. James realised he couldn't get in because the gates were closed. They slowly opened and both vehicles parked at the front of the house. James and Juliet headed for the front door. James watched the gates close. He went to unlock the door and discovered there was no keyhole. They heard a voice saying access granted and the front door opened. They both entered. Juliet was carrying Roger, who suddenly decided to say dad, dad, mom, mom. Juliet immediately kissed him on the cheek and so did James, he'd never heard him say that before.

Their home looked beautiful and pristine, they looked in every room. When they came to the fourth bedroom the door had been replaced with something far more substantial. Juliet tried to enter, there was no door handle they heard a voice again, access was granted and the door unlocked. Juliet pushed it open nervously, wondering what she was going to find. There were computers and screens everywhere with a very large plasma screen attached to one wall. James estimated there must have been over £1 million worth of equipment in this one room. James looked in the far corner, seeing a playpen with a surveillance camera pointing directly into it. He tapped Juliet's arm and she turned around and smiled.

Mary appeared on the plasma screen. "Good morning Juliet and James, how do you like your new office Juliet? This is where you will work while James is on missions and once you have given birth to my new godchild," she emphasised, "and got yourself back into shape, we may let you go with James on some missions."

James and Juliet were speechless, Roger waved to Mary on the screen. Mary looked around herself and quickly waved back, not wishing the other agents to see her respond to Roger and lose her street cred.

Juliet could monitor the whole property from her station the gate every part of the house including the garden, plus every room. Mary was leaving nothing to chance. Mary continued, "In the event there is a power cut this is what will happen, don't be alarmed."

Mary turned to someone who was not on view and nodded. The power was cut to the house, the lights went out in the room and the shutters started coming down immediately on the windows; within a few seconds the generator cut in, the power was restored, and Mary appeared on the plasma screen again as if nothing had happened.

"While you're in this room, Juliet, it doesn't matter what happens to the rest of the property. You and the children will be safe along with the thousands of pounds worth of equipment we have installed."

"Why have you gone to all the expense, Mary? You have the same equipment where you are."

Mary vanished from the screen and suddenly walked into the room. James pulled his gun immediately, placing it against Mary's forehead, not convinced it was really her. With a flick of her hand she had removed the gun from James's hand commenting, "Boys and their toys," smiling. She continued: "You're lucky I didn't break your other arm, James."

They all went into the living room. Mary made everyone a coffee, which was rather surprising. She returned with a tray of refreshments and seated herself by Juliet on the settee. "You are aware we've had many security issues this year, attempts on my life and on yours. We have a serious leak in the system somewhere and we need help to find out who it is. We have set you up with an independent station. With a code on my phone I can disconnect you from the system so you can operate independently, if necessary, and retain vital secrets in your servers." Mary took a sip of her coffee. "You are the only two agents I trust completely, although, James, you do have a habit of bending the rules, but for all the right reasons," she smiled.

Juliet and James leaned back, relieved at the explanation they had received, it all made sense now.

Mary insisted. "You will both have to be micro-chipped, I'm afraid that includes Roger, that way I personally can track your every movement and not the organisation; sorry, that's a mistake, what I should have said is me and Juliet are the only two people that can track you until you, James, dispose of the rogue agent or agents."

Juliet glanced to James and held his hand.

"James will be travelling a lot Juliet, you will have to trust him. You can monitor his whereabouts at all times along with me."

Juliet quickly responded: "What do you mean, trust him?" Her expression was solemn.

"I'm teaming him up with various agents who I suspect are rogue but have no real proof."

"You don't expect him to sleep with female agents, do you, Mary?" Juliet asked.

"That shouldn't be necessary, James has my sanction to execute any agent if he has absolute proof they are betraying the organisation. Although I would prefer them alive, James, to question further once you have the evidence."

Juliet stared at James for reassurance he wouldn't go to bed with a female agent in pursuit of the truth, with tears in her eyes.

Mary changed the subject. "The doctor is coming tomorrow to remove your plasters from your arm and leg you should be fine then and fully operational again." Mary kissed Roger on the forehead and left.

Juliet made another drink, returning to the settee and James. Roger was crawling around on the carpet playing with his toys. "James promise me you won't sleep with another woman, I don't think I could stand it not now."

"Definitely not, I'll shoot the bitch first whoever she is," James reassured.

Juliet hugged him, "You will be careful James I don't want to lose you."

James was deep in thought and came to the conclusion the only place the information could be leaking from was head office itself. A field agent wouldn't have access to some of the sensitive information held on the firm's computers.

Chapter 17

Seek and Destroy

Early the next morning the doctor arrived and removed James's plaster casts. He scratched his leg furiously and then his arm, going into the shower to freshen up. When he returned he saw the doctor injecting Juliet's thigh with a microchip. He instructed James to drop his trousers and he did the same to him. Juliet held Roger. The doctor smeared some cream on Roger's thigh, and then eased the microchip under the skin Roger didn't flinch in the slightest; he hadn't felt a thing, unlike James and Juliet. The doctor left.

Juliet picked up Roger, heading for her workstation with James closely following. She turned on her monitor and a map appeared of the British Isles. She could see three continuing flashes, each with a name beside them indicating exactly where they were. Juliet smiled, commenting, "You try and cheat on me buster and I'll blow your balls off."

James laughed, "As if I would, love."

The next morning James drove to London, pulling into the yard and going into the office, pressing the button on the wall allowing him into the control room, the heart of the operations centre. Mary glanced up. Seeing James scanning the operatives, she knew he was on a mission she had set for him.

James went behind the computers, crawling between the workstations and the wall. Everybody looked nervous, the female staff wearing skirts stood up. James continued along the wall until he'd reached the end. James went to stand up and banged his head on the table just in time to see whoever was sitting at the desk drop a memory stick.

James drew his gun only to discover the person sitting at the workstation was John, an agent he had trusted. Mary pulled her gun aiming for John; he put his hands up quickly: "I've done nothing wrong," he pleaded. James moved around to the front of the workstation plastered in dust and cobwebs retrieving the memory stick from the floor. John ran for the door and James shot him in the leg without hesitation. Two other agents cuffed John and led him away to receive treatment for his wound.

Mary placed the memory stick in the computer and found top-secret files had been downloaded. She removed the memory stick from the computer, turning and patting James on the shoulder: "How did you know James?" Mary asked, leading him into her office.

"I thought about it last night. It had to be someone who had access to the main computers. The information the terrorists were retrieving was very accurate, no terrorist organisation could be that lucky, being in the right place at the right time."

"I wonder if he has any accomplices," Mary suggested.

"Let's find out, Mary, where is he?" James asked.

Mary showed James to the interrogation room. "Let me deal with him."

James went into the interrogation room; Mary watched from behind the glass. She was horrified to see James remove the knife strapped to his leg. She watched as James grabbed John by the hair, sticking the knife under his chin. He then slashed John's ear, blood was pouring everywhere. It was not long before John was spilling the beans of who he was working for. Under normal circumstances Mary would not allow any person to be treated in this manner. However, national security had been jeopardised and she needed to know who the enemy was, whatever the cost.

John then made a fatal mistake by owning up to shooting Jackie with a different gun trying to make out it was a terrorist attack. Mary covered her eyes she knew what was coming and she couldn't stop him even if she wanted to. James drew his knife slowly across John's throat, the blood spurted all over the observation window. James left the interrogation room after wiping his knife clean on John's suit along with his hands.

Mary shouted at him, "My office now, James!"

James sat down in the chair "I understand why you did what you did James. It's not very professional, you're just lucky we retrieved the information from him first, otherwise you would have been in real trouble with me."

"Sorry, Mary, the thought of him shooting Jackie just lit my fuse."

"Go home James, while I decide what we do next regarding the other three agents, although I suspect the only cure will be for you to eliminate them. At least we know who the traitors are now, thanks to you."

James left the office and drove steadily home realising John who he trusted to look after Jackie had taken her life. He hadn't felt for a long time the hollow feeling of losing a loved one. Which made him realise how much more precious Juliet was to him now.

He also realised why Mary had gone to such lengths to protect him and Juliet. He parked outside the gates, waiting for them to open. Juliet came over the intercom. "Have you been faithful to me, husband?" she chuckled.

"Of course you silly cow, let me in."

Juliet opened the gates. James parked and went into the house; he explained to Juliet everything that had taken place and what he'd done to John. "You're beginning to frighten me James, you don't think twice about killing anyone."

Mary appeared on the plasma screen. "That's why he's alive and others die, because he's quick and efficient, don't scold him for doing his job Juliet."

"Okay boss." The plasma screen went blank.

Juliet glanced to one of the monitors. "Who's that standing at the gate James?"

Juliet and James watched the person trying to see around the corner not realising he was being monitored. James commented. "Probably a nosy neighbour, if it was an agent or a terrorist they'd know they were being monitored and wouldn't stand there in full view."

James's parents pulled up outside the gates. Juliet opened the gates; James's parents drove in and parked beside Juliet's car. They went to the front door carrying a large parcel; they watched James's father trying to find the doorbell or a door handle, which made them both smile. Juliet release the door and it opened they walked in nervously. "Hello, hello is anybody here, James, Juliet, hello."

James couldn't resist, he pressed the intercom button. "Don't move you're surrounded." Mrs Thompson dropped the parcel her hands in the air and so did Mr Thompson. James came into the hallway in stitches laughing at them both. "That wasn't funny son, you could have frightened your mother to death," he continued, "This is like Fort Knox." Juliet came from her workstation carrying Roger and joined them in the living room. Mrs Thompson placed the box on the coffee table and embraced Juliet and

Roger together, kissing Roger and then Juliet on the cheek. Juliet finally felt accepted. Mrs Thompson placed the box on the floor, guiding Roger to open it.

They watched Roger tearing away at the wrapping paper. Without warning Mary spoke, "James! The toy's booby-trapped, take it outside quickly. James pushed Roger over, grabbing the box and running outside. There was a small explosion, no more than the sound of a shot gun cartridge. The toy shattered into pieces and a slither of plastic stuck in James's leg.

Juliet had scooped Roger up from the floor Mrs Thompson had fainted and Mr Thompson was comforting her wondering what the hell is gone on. Roger had a slight bump on his forehead from where James had pushed him out of the way. Juliet comforted him till he stopped crying.

James limped into the living room Juliet thrust Roger into Mr Thompson's hands. "Hold him," were her instructions. She grabbed the first-aid box from the kitchen, returning to James. His father watched Juliet pull the piece of plastic from James's leg and quickly bandage the wound. Mary spoke again, "The doctor is on the way."

"How can you live like this, son?"

James responded "This is nothing, just an everyday occurrence in our lives, we are agents and we have to expect the unexpected all the time."

Juliet took Roger from Mr Thompson as Mrs Thompson came round and burst into tears: "I nearly killed my grandson," she sobbed. She took Roger from Juliet, hugging him.

"Don't worry, mother, father, no one was hurt, that's the main thing, and I only have a scratch. The doctor will soon be here and fix me up. More importantly, where did you buy the toy from for Roger?"

"You know how your mother loves to do competitions James. She won it in a competition, according to the man who delivered it, although your mother couldn't remember entering the competition, she just presumed she had forgotten."

Mary's voice was heard. "Take them both into the control room, Juliet. I need to see them and speak to them." Mr and Mrs Thompson looked around the room to see where the voice was coming from.

They followed Juliet and James to the control room and gasped at all the equipment they saw, not understanding what half of it was of course. Mary appeared on the screen; she smiled politely, and explained they must never accept anything for James's family, without having solid proof of where it had come from. She also explained how important James was to national security, and under no circumstances were they to mention what they've just seen.

Mr Thompson spoke, "We can only apologise, Mary, we didn't realise, we just didn't think anything of receiving a toy, which we thought was suitable for Roger our grandson." Juliet had passed Roger to James and was comforting Mrs Thompson, who was still in shock, and crying.

Mary finally commented: "You must both realise that Juliet and James have very important jobs in securing the safety of the country. You should both be very proud of your son and his accomplishments, I'm very proud to have him on my team and as a friend, someone we can trust without question."

"We are extremely proud of him, Mary, our only regret is, not believing him when he said he didn't rape that girl."

"Believe it or not, you did him a big favour and me as well, otherwise he wouldn't be working for me now," Mary concluded, and the plasma screen went blank.

They all returned to the living room. Juliet poured a small whiskey for Margaret, James's mother.

"I wouldn't mind one either Juliet please," James's father asked, sitting beside his wife and placing his arm around her shoulder to try and comfort her.

"Please don't repeat anything you've heard and seen, what we do and how we operate; with Juliet pregnant security is essential to us all."

His parents agreed and said they were looking forward to having another grandchild in the family. The doctor arrived and attended to James's leg, just three of four stitches to seal the wound, and a plaster. Mr and Mrs Thompson left, first kissing Juliet on the cheek and then their son. "It looks that they have accepted me as your wife, James, I'm so relieved they like me now, it will make life so much better for us."

James went outside and collected all the evidence from the exploding toy he could find and placed it in his van to take to London for more examination. He left early the next morning and arrived at the headquarters parking in the yard.

Mary was there to greet him, taking the evidence from him for forensics to look at. She was deeply concerned someone was trying now to target Roger; children had never come into the equation before, which was a disturbing development. Perhaps the terrorists or whoever they were, hoped by injuring Roger they would get to James and making him more careless and an easier target for them to eliminate permanently.

James waited for several hours while forensics went over the evidence. He was finally called into Mary's office; she made him a coffee and he sat at the other side of her desk. "Interesting James, forensics found a partial fingerprint which matches that of one of our agents. That now makes three agents with links to a terrorist group, most likely the remnants of Khan's organisation."

"Who are they and where are they, Mary? I will dispose of them immediately," James said, sipping his coffee as if he was just going to the shop to buy cigarettes.

Mary smiled at his response: "You are the most dangerous, calculating agent I've ever controlled; Juliet is right, you are frightening, you fear absolutely nothing."

"Come on, let's get on with it," James said impatiently. "I want to be home for supper." he smiled.

Mary shook her head in disbelief. "One of the agents is in Ireland, one in Malta, which will be a problem, and the other is in Amsterdam."

"Yes, I see what you mean, Malta will be a problem. I will have to grow my beard back and let my hair grow long again."

"No need James, we would just give you false passports for yourself and Juliet, I can't risk you taking Roger this time."

"Definitely not, Mary, do I have to go with Juliet? Can't I go on my own?" he questioned.

"It always looks better if you go with a partner, customs and the police are less suspicious, as you know. We've already upset them once this year and they won't take kindly to having a repeat episode on their doorstep, especially as some of the forces over there are sympathetic to the religious fanatics."

"Where shall I leave Roger? I know my parents would have him but now's there's been the attempt on his life, that would be like giving them the key to the door."

"I will have Roger while you're away, it will only be for a day or two at the most," she said smiling.

"You can't turn him into an agent yet Mary, he is too young," James joked.

"If he's anything like his father God help the world," she said standing up continuing. "Go home, James, I'll be in touch when we have all the necessary paperwork ready for you to travel to the various countries. I must confess I am rather concerned regarding sending Juliet with you, but she's the only other agent I really trust in the organisation at the moment."

James drove home and explained everything to Juliet; she was rather excited with the thought of having an adventure at long last after sitting in an office.

She was three months pregnant and starting to show, but felt she could still move quickly if she had to in an emergency. James on the other hand, was not at all convinced Juliet would cope in a firefight if everything went tits up.

Three days later James received the phone call he been waiting for to mobilise. Juliet packed everything for Roger she could think of and overnight bags for herself and James. She checked both their handguns to make sure they were clean and fully operational.

They took a steady ride to London, turning into the yard and going into Mary's office, where she immediately took Roger from Juliet, sitting him on her desk, allowing him to play with all her pens and paperwork, a mess she certainly wouldn't relish cleaning up after he'd finished.

Mary pointed to the settee at the back of office. "You wear that at all times Juliet." She looked across to the settee seeing a Kevlar bullet-proof full-length vest. "Go and put it on, Juliet, now or you don't go with James."

Juliet protested, "I'll look six months pregnant wearing that Mary, my figure is bad enough now."

"Do as you are told," James said sternly, "Or I'm not taking you with me."

Juliet reluctantly slid the vest over her bra, it came right down to the bottom of her stomach and she was fully protected. James smiled with approval. Mary had gone the extra mile to protect his wife in a potentially dangerous situation.

"Your instructions are," Mary said calmly, "there is a helicopter waiting for you at the airport. You will be flown into Ireland while you deal with the first agent. The helicopter will refuel and then fly you to Amsterdam to your second mission. From there you will board the helicopter again for Malta. There is one of our aircraft carriers in the port and the helicopter will drop you off there. You can complete your third assignment. You will then drive a short distance to the old disused aerodrome used in World

War Two. There will be a small aeroplane waiting for you there to take you out of the country. There's nothing else for me to tell you two other than Godspeed and good luck and please come home safe."

They drove to the airport and boarded the helicopter flying to Ireland; it was just turning dusk as they arrived; a car was waiting for them to use. They decided Juliet would drive and they made their way through the narrow lanes to an address out in the countryside where the rogue agent was supposed to live.

James told Juliet to park a little way up the road and to wait there for him. James cut across the field and approached the house from the back. He fitted his silencer to his gun; he heard a dog bark, and the outside light came on. James sat patiently using his night vision binoculars. He could see the agent to be eliminated. He was rather concerned he was too far away and thought he'd have to risk the shot, considering the dog had alerted the agent.

James aimed and fired twice. The next thing he realised was that the dog was coming straight for him and grabbed his arm. James put his gun to the dog's head and pulled the trigger. The Alsatian dropped dead. James ran towards the house and could see the agent on the floor still moving. James put another two bullets in his head to finish him off.

He could hear a woman screaming in the house as he ran back across the field to where Juliet was waiting for him. He jumped in the car and she drove off for the airport to rejoin the helicopter with the engine running waiting for them. They boarded quickly. Juliet noticed blood running down James's arm from where the Alsatian had bit him.

She bandaged him as best she could, using the first-aid kit aboard. He quickly changed his top so no one could see the ripped garment where the dog had attacked him. They cuddled each other in the back of the military helicopter, it certainly wasn't warm. A short while later they landed at a military base. Again a car was provided and Juliet drove, as she was used to driving in foreign countries. James checked his firearm and made sure he had plenty of spare ammo.

Juliet said, "Be careful my love, don't do anything silly," kissing him on the cheek. James ran up the flight of stairs in the block of flats. Concealing his weapon he reached number 20, the flat where the agent lived. James drew his gun and entered the premises to see the agent sitting in a chair holding his young son, not much older than Roger. James didn't want to shoot with a child so close to the target.

James hesitated only for a few seconds and the rogue agent pulled his gun and shot James in the arm. James fired back immediately, hitting the agent in the forehead and killing him instantly. James ran out of the building hearing the child's mother screaming at the top of her voice as he ran. James jumped into the car and Juliet drove off quickly returning to the military base. "You will have to bandage my arm love, I have been shot," he said as they boarded the helicopter.

Juliet examined the wound. The bullet had gone straight through, which was good news. She placed the bandage as tight as she could. The helicopter took off; James leaned with his back against the steel bodywork, picturing the child's face as he shot his father, it reminded him so much of Roger. He realised if the shoe was on the other foot any other agent would have done exactly the same in the interests of his country's security.

James explained to Juliet why he'd been shot. Her eyes filled with tears: "I couldn't take the shot James, not with a child involved. I'll deal with the last agent, James, you're in no shape to continue," she said with conviction.

"Over my dead body love, there's still plenty of fight left in me yet, you drive the vehicles I'll deal with the problem," he smiled, kissing her on the cheek reassuringly. They didn't arrive in Malta till daybreak, landing on the aircraft carrier.

James was escorted to the medic on board who took a closer look at his wound, tidying up the damage and giving him some painkillers to help him complete his mission.

The captain was rather concerned, there appeared to be more police officers patrolling the docks than usual. James changed into a sailor's uniform to make it easier for him to leave the ship. Juliet was given an armful of empty folders to make it look as she was an official.

They left the ship watching the police in front of them. They were stopped immediately: "Passport." Juliet showed hers to the officer. He told them to continue. James decided to leave the hire car where it was in case the police had been tipped off. They took a local bus to St Paul's Bay.

Mary phoned and Juliet answered. "I think you may have to abort," Mary suggested, "from the chatter we're hearing on the airwaves someone has tipped them off." James took the phone from Juliet. "I'm not quitting now," he said, and he turned the phone off.

Not Guilty

Mary phoned again: "This is a direct order abort, abort." James saw the agent they were looking for go into an alleyway. He quickly screwed his silencer to the end of the barrel and ran as quickly as he could into the alleyway just in time to see the agent start to ascend the stairs.

James shot him twice in the back of the head and he dropped. James dismantled his gun, returning to Juliet, who was still talking to Mary. James grabbed the phone: "Mission completed, coming home," and he rang off.

James flagged down a taxi asking him to taking to the docks to where HMS Churchill was docked. The police officers watched James and Juliet board the aircraft carrier, at least they were now on British territory again. The next problem was getting home before all hell broke loose. James phoned Mary and explained their predicament. She advised him she would take care of everything as usual.

The helicopter was refuelled they'd come in on. They boarded, heading for Gibraltar, landing a short while later. James and Juliet were absolutely knackered. Mary had arranged for a private jet to fly them back to London. The flight home seemed uneventful to start with, although James was not overly keen on the stewardess, she seemed nervous and twitchy.

Before James had chance to react the stewardess pulled a handgun and shot Juliet in the shoulder. James returned fire, killing the woman instantly. James went to see the pilot and explained what had happened. He conveyed the information to Mary.

James returned to Juliet who was bruised but unharmed thanks to Mary making her wear the bullet-proof vest. They landed, a car was waiting for them; on the way back to the yard, James had the driver pull over by a flower stand. He purchased a large bouquet of flowers for Mary, which he presented on their arrival. Mary blushed;, she hadn't been given flowers since her husband had died. They all went into her office.

"I don't know what to say James, obviously thank you for the flowers, what you to have done for our country in the last 24 hours is remarkable."

James suddenly realised Roger was missing he looked around, "Where's Roger?" he asked hurriedly.

Mary laughed, pressing the button on the wall giving them access to the heart of the operation. There were agents playing with Roger. Seeing James and Juliet, they all stood up and clapped in appreciation of his accomplishment for the agency.

Juliet retrieved Roger; Mary looked to James with a more serious expression. "I hear you were shot, why? What happened?"

James explained, Mary shook her head, "I've never been in that position James and I don't know how I would react either. I can't imagine what was going through your mind."

James sighed: "I will never forget the expression on the child's face as I shot his father, that's something I will have to live with for the rest of my life," he said, taking Roger from Juliet and kissing him on the cheek.

"I see you found another mole on the aeroplane, you were very lucky you both weren't killed," she smiled.

"Go home and rest, your car is in the yard and refilled. Drive carefully, please, you have my godson with you."

They left the office and James drove, finally reaching home at daybreak. Roger was already fast asleep in the car seat. Juliet put him to bed and they retired themselves, not waking till late in the afternoon.

Chapter 18

New Arrival

James and Juliet were starting to live a normal family life for a change. The terrorist threat, although always present, had calmed down for the time being. The agency seemed to be free of rogue agents or they were being very careful.

Roger had found his feet and was ploughing around the bungalow like a steam train, causing havoc wherever he went. Juliet went into hospital; she had gone into labour. Roger was staying with his grandparents while they awaited the new arrival.

Juliet was calling James every name under the sun as she endured an eight-hour labour, assuring him she would castrate him the minute she left hospital and she was never going to have sex again for as long as she lived.

Finally, she gave birth to a daughter who they both decided to name Fiona Mary Thompson. Juliet was taken to the ward for observation overnight, before she would be released. Mary in her wisdom, had assigned an agent to stay in the corridor, just to ensure her new goddaughter was safe. Mary was tickled pink because they had used two of her names. She was a very proud godmother.

James collected Juliet and their daughter from the hospital the following morning, after being given a clean bill of health. They wondered how the midwife would take to entering Fort Knox as his parents had nicknamed their home. Juliet had placed a cot by the side of their bed to look after Fiona for the first few weeks, until she was happy with her progress.

Roger was introduced to his new sister, who he wanted to play with immediately, and was very annoyed when he wasn't allowed to. Mary drove down from London to see her new godchild and was overwhelmed that she was allowed to feed her while Juliet and James tried to control Roger. They hoped the novelty would soon wear off and Roger would just carry on playing with his toys and eventually ignore his sister until she was a little older. After a couple of hours Mary left to return to London to direct operations.

Juliet left James with Fiona, their daughter, and went to her workstation to catch up on events although Mary had briefed both of them. Juliet just wanted to make sure there was no chatter on the airwaves. Juliet called James to her. She'd caught the end of a conversation relating to Stratford theatre and explosives planted to cause maximum devastation.

London was the normal target for terrorists, they had come to realise London was no longer such an easy target, so had spread their wings to less secure areas to wreak havoc. Juliet contacted Mary; she instructed James to go and investigate and not be afraid to use his security card if anyone tried to stop him; they would have to answer to her.

James handed his daughter to Juliet leaving her to wrestle with two children and keep control of events. Juliet made James wear his earpiece so she could talk to him, which James detested wearing, he said it ruined his concentration; he wasn't a woman and couldn't do two things at once, which made Juliet laugh.

James drove to the theatre, parked his van, checked his firearm and concealed it beneath his coat. He flashed his card at the door and immediately was allowed in. Hee searched underneath the staging and the tiered seating finally coming across as sealed crate. He used his knife and prised one of the boards free only to see explosives. He ran across to the wall and pressed the fire alarm. The theatre immediately started to evacuate. James then phoned Mary who relayed the information to the bomb squad and the local police.

James vacated the building when he was stopped by a detective. James showed him his card. The detective phoned the number. James watched the detective's expression turn white, whatever Mary was saying to him had obviously had some affect. He quickly returned the card to James and walked off. James jumped in his van as a bomb squad arrived. Mary came over the intercom. "Sorry about that, James, I don't think that detective will bother you in the future."

"Thanks Mary, as always, for protecting my arse."

"James, look out for any suspicious characters. I suspect they'd probably stand the other side of the river in the playing fields. Drive round and see if you can spot anybody and report back to me before you shoot anyone please, unless you are threatened."

James drove across the bridge and parked his van. James scanned the field and could see nothing out of place; two mothers playing with their children. He continued walking along the riverbank, noticing one secluded fisherman had no fishing line in his rod. The fishermen started to dial on his mobile. James drew his gun and shot the mobile out of the man's hand, allowing it to fall in the water.

The fishermen got up to run and James shot him in the leg and handcuffed him. The local police were swarming all round him within minutes including police marksmen. They made James drop his gun until they realised who he worked for, then he was immediately released. James retrieved his gun; he could hear Mary's voice speaking to one of the officers, who gave the impression she was going to wet herself any minute, the way she was shouting.

James returned to his van and headed for home, explaining to Mary on the way where the mobile was so it could be retrieved for further examination. James thought it was odd being above the law, or it appeared that way to him anyway.

Juliet scolded him immediately "I told you to wear your earpiece." He removed it from his ear. "It doesn't bloody work, don't blame me," he snarled.

Juliet examined the earpiece. "It helps my love if you switch it on," she smiled smugly, rocking her daughter.

James poked his tongue out at "Know it all."

Juliet clipped him round the ear as he walked in, passing his daughter to him saying, "I put Roger to bed, he is being a pain in the arse."

"I suspect he's jealous, after all you always used to give him your attention and now...."

"Are you accusing me of not loving Roger James, if you are, I think you're being grossly unfair to me," she scolded.

"Hey, I wasn't saying anything Juliet, get off your high horse or are you starting to suffer from postnatal depression?"

"How would you know what postnatal depression is? You haven't the brains, you probably couldn't even spell the word."

James stood up carefully, passing his daughter to her Juliet. He calmly went into Roger's bedroom, wrapping him in a blanket he lifted him from his bed, and went out of the door. Taking Juliet's car, he drove to his parents. They greeted him at the door rather surprised: "What's the matter, son?"

"Juliet's in a bit of a strop and I thought if you would look after Roger for a few days, it might just ease the tension, it's a lot for her to cope with and work."

James's mother took Roger and put him to bed; his father poured him a small Scotch. "I understand, son, your mother was all over the place when she gave birth to you. Thank God you were our only child, I couldn't have gone through it all again," he smiled, patting James on the back.

James smiled, "thanks for the info dad, I suppose I better finish my drink and face the firing squad that awaits me."

His father joked, "Just don't shoot her son it won't improve the situation at all."

James pulled up to the gates waiting for them to open and they didn't. He phoned Juliet and she wasn't picking up the phone. He phoned the office and they released the gates for him. He parked the car and went inside, after control released the locks for him.

Juliet was sitting on the edge of the settee crying. Mary was talking to her over the intercom telling her not to be so stupid and pull herself together. James wondered whether that was helping matters or not. He could hear his daughter crying in the other room; he went in and fetched her, making a bottle and sitting down in the chair feeding her.

Juliet occasionally glanced to him, seeing James playing with his daughter just like he did with Roger; he didn't distinguish between the two children whatsoever. Juliet felt lonely and not wanted by James or her daughter, which she knew in her own mind was a stupid thing to think, but she couldn't help the way she felt. Perhaps James was right, she may be suffering from postnatal depression..

Whatever it was, she didn't like it and wanted it fixed immediately. She picked up her mobile and rang the organisation's doctor who agreed to come out and see her tonight. She didn't bother to talk to James, she felt she may just start another argument and she didn't want her marriage to end; as much as she hated him at this precise second, she knew she really loved him; so much confusion.

Not Guilty

Juliet opened the gates for the doctor to drive in and greeted him at the front door, leading him in to the living room. Juliet asked James politely, "Would you leave us please I want to talk to the doctor privately."

James nodded and went in to his bedroom and after winding is daughter, he placed in the cot on Juliet's side of the bed. He sat there quietly watching the television, with no sound on trying not to disturb Fiona his daughter. The doctor opened the bedroom door asking James to join them in the living room. He sat quietly in the armchair knowing there was something wrong and had no idea how to fix it.

The doctor addressed them both, "Juliet's symptoms are quite normal, her hormones are all over the place. So you James, will have to tolerate and understand when Juliet loses the plot. Within a month thing should settle down. If they don't I will start to administer treatment; hopefully that will not be necessary, one last thing Juliet I must ask you for your gun, in your state of mind I don't consider you fit to handle one."

Juliet handed over her gun without a murmur. The doctor passed it to James. "James, keep it safe so she can't get access until I am satisfied she is in the correct state of mind."

Juliet started to cry again, feeling her world was collapsing around her. This was the last thing James expected he would have to deal with. It's bad enough being shot at, but to have a wife that may shoot you, as well, or your daughteris rather alarming. James showed the doctor to the door, shook his hand and say goodbye.

James returned to Juliet and placed his arm around her shoulder. "Why didn't you talk to me love before you got in this state?"

Juliet shrugged her shoulders, "I don't know, I don't understand, I'm all confused."

James helped Juliet to bed and he returned to the living room where he decided he would sleep tonight. He didn't think Juliet would harm her daughter so he left her in there asking control to turn the camera on in his bedroom and monitor Juliet and to wake him if there was an issue, but to be sure to turn the camera off if she was undressing.

James quietly phoned Mary and explained the situation. James suggested that she was locked out of her workstation until she settled down. Mary agreed, as director I can't risk her with sensitive information, if there's any chance she could blow a fuse.

James then phoned his mother who had suffered similar symptoms. She was only too pleased to be of any help to Juliet, she would come over first thing in the morning. It was barely daybreak when his mother arrived. James carefully removed his daughter from her cot, not wishing to wake Juliet.

His mother took charge immediately changing and feeding Fiona. Juliet finally made an appearance around 10 o'clock in the morning and sat on the settee, still in the clothes she was wearing yesterday. James's mother went over and sat by her, after making them both a coffee.

She explained to Juliet how she felt when she gave birth to James. Juliet smiled realising there was someone else in the world who understood how she felt. James didn't interfere, he just went about his business, going into their control room and talking to the operatives in London. James just prayed he wouldn't be sent on an operation until Juliet was better.

James received a call from the Mary; he was needed in Bristol there was believed to be a container carrying terrorists and explosives due to dock in four hours. James thought, Beam me up Scotty, I don't need this crap, not now. James agreed to go; returning to the living room he asked his mother if she would stay till he returned home. She looked very worried, knowing he was going on a mission. Juliet glanced up to him smiling. "Your mother is great, she understands how I feel James. I'll be okay, you go, be careful, I love you."

James kissed them both on the forehead and went out of the door. Jumping in his van, he drove to Bristol docks, parking up out of sight. The ship had just docked. James showed his card and was allowed to board the vessel. There were only three containers on deck which simplified matters. Two had seals on the locks the third one had been broken. James could hear police sirens and cars approaching, he appreciated the backup although it might be too late.

James opened the door slowly to find the container empty. The crew wanted to disembark and James refused to let them, drawing his gun to make sure they knew he meant business, and displaying his badge of authority. Two police cars pulled up alongside the ship and 4 armed police officers joined him, handcuffing 6 crew members and the captain. The police officers and James started searching the ship. Suddenly there was gunfire. James ran towards the sound which echoed through the bowels of the ship.

He came across a wounded officer and seeing the head of a terrorist peeping over pipes,, he put a bullet straight in his head. The other police

Not Guilty

officers joined him, radioing for an ambulance. James led the way, weaving his way around an engine room the size of a cathedral.

James heard a noise, looked behind him and the officer saw a man walking along a pipe with a machine gun; before he had chance to fire, James took him out and he came crashing to the floor with a thud, splitting his head in half on a piece of steel. They continued working their way through the engine room and found no one else. They returned to the deck. James broke the seals on the other two containers, finding them full of explosives. The officer shook his hand and thanked him for his assistance and James left them to it to clear up the mess.

James started homeward bound, receiving a message from Mary on how proud she was of his professional approach and hoped Juliet would soon recover and become one of the team again. James went to walk in the front door. It opened and Juliet threw her arms around his shoulders kissing him passionately on the lips. "I feel wonderful James; your mother is marvellous."

James entered the living room to see his mother feeding his daughter, a very happy woman and pleased she could help. Perhaps she felt it would go some way to mending the damage they had inflicted on James some time ago.

Juliet commented: "I now have a mother again, someone I can talk to and love." She hugged James's mother who smiled broadly with satisfaction that she'd been of help.

James sat and thought to himself. Perhaps all Juliet needed was a mother; something she hadn't had since she was 15. She'd had no one to turn to in her life. She'd obviously buried herself in her work, trying to find a distraction from the pain she had suffered. Perhaps they both were kindred spirits; he decided no matter what happened he knew he would always love her.

"I'll make the tea Margaret," Juliet said dashing into the kitchen with an enthusiasm James hadn't seen for a long time. There was actually a spring in her step. Juliet started preparing food for everyone. James received a phone call from the Mary. "The Prime Minister has asked me to convey his thanks to you for all the missions you have carried out on the country's behalf. He is recommending you for an MBE, unfortunately James you will not be able to be publicly recognised, so it will have to be a very private affair."

"Thank you Mary, you could always give me a pay rise too," he joked.

"Goodbye James, look after my godchildren otherwise you will have me to answer to young man."

Juliet ran over and embraced James. "You deserve it husband, you dance with the devil every day and still you come home to a miserable wife."

"I don't mind, love, you're good practice on how to deal with terrorists," hee joked. Juliet punched him in the ribs then kissed him on the lips. "If only I had my gun James," she laughed.

"You won't get that back until you're, really nice to me." Juliet returned to the kitchen and continued making sandwiches for everyone. Margaret, James's mother, went into the bedroom with Fiona placing her in the cot.

She returned to the living room to enjoy the sandwiches Juliet had made. Then excused herself an hour later to go home, telling Juliet to ring her any time she wanted to talk or come over and see her whichever she preferred.

Juliet walked her to the door and they hugged each other. Juliet stayed there waving goodbye until James's mother was out of sight. She came back into the living room jumping on James's lap, placing her arms around his neck.

* * *

Juliet continued to recover from her postnatal depression and within a couple of months everything seemed to be back to normal. She had been given her gun back and was allowed into the control room again. Mary frequently visited; monitoring her new God daughter Fiona. They knew it wouldn't be long before they were called back into action.

Chapter 19

Back on the road again

Mary turned up unannounced with a very worried expression. "James, Juliet," she said sitting down on the settee taking Fiona from Juliet's arms commenting, "you're both taking a holiday and Fiona is staying with me, your parents are going to look after Roger while you're away."

James and Juliet looked at each other and at Mary, "going where Mary?" James asked earnestly.

"I have a very specially designed motorhome on its way to you and bloody expensive to make, so don't bend it James. I want you both to travel to Scotland, we believe there is a terrorist organisation forming, allowed into the country by our own governments stupidity they obviously came in posing as immigrants."

James sighed. "Here we go again."

Juliet glanced at Fiona then lifted her eyes to Mary. "Where do we start to look?"

"Good question you've heard the chatter yourself Juliet. We suspect they could be anywhere between Nairn and Poolewe, trying to find a location suitable to hide a large quantity of explosives coming in from the Middle East."

Juliet cuddled Fiona. "How long before we have to leave?"

Mary glanced to her watch. "About an hour get packed," she said without compassion.

Juliet reluctantly handed Fiona to Mary and went off into the bedroom to pack. James suspected there was a little more to the situation than Mary was letting on, otherwise she would have allowed them to take the children. "Okay Mary how serious is the situation?"

James watched Mary's expression fall away to one of business. "Very dangerous James, don't underestimate the people you are taking on. That's why I couldn't allow the children to travel with you." She sighed heavily, "If there were any other agents as good as you and Juliet I would have sent them I can assure you."

James tried to produce a reassuring smile although in the back of his mind he loved his children dearly, he wished he hadn't had any at all. When he was single he only had to worry about himself. Juliet returned to the room just as a large motorhome parked outside the gates. Juliet stared at the monitor looking at the vehicle which appeared to be more like a luxury coach than a motorhome she had envisaged they would be receiving. Mary escorted them to the vehicle which towered above them all. No door handles smoked glass. Mary touched the side of the motorhome and the door opened they entered. Mary explained to them how it all worked; she would press a button on a cabinet and out would pop a computer along with the workstation similar to the one they had in the bungalow. Mary explained, "you see the red button on the dashboard along with all the cameras which monitor the exterior of the vehicle when you press that button the whole vehicle will lift from the ground on Jacks, which will give you access to the car."

Mary watched Juliet's expression broaden noticing on one of the cameras the car was a Lamborghini something she wanted for a long time and are favourite colour black. "Don't get too excited Juliet the car is not a toy and before you smash anything up you two I just want you to realise you will have over £2 million worth of equipment at your disposal. The Prime Minister would not be a happy bunny if you destroy these vehicles."

Mary then pressed another button on the dashboard; a cabinet at the far end of the motorhome revolved displaying an Arsenal equipped for world War three including rocket launchers. "Like all our vehicles this one will protect itself from intruders with the added ability to target and shoot any vehicles from the front or the rear and all the tyres are bullet-proof so in theory the vehicle is virtually indestructible but I'm sure you two will prove us wrong with your reputation," Mary smiled taking Fiona out of the motorhome. "Oh I almost forgot," Mary commented, "here are two

PSV licences in case you're pulled over by the police, now on your way and be careful."

James sat behind the wheel; the whole vehicle was massive. Before James could touch anything, the motorhome started itself. Juliet sat in the passenger seat hearing a voice say, "Your destination James? I suggest Dunbar as your first stopover?" James and Juliet just stared at each other. Juliet quickly asked,

"Who are you or what are you?"

"I'm the heart of the vehicle I control everything I can even drive for you I am totally automated and interfaced."

"What do we call you," James asked?"

"Do you want to know my technical name?"

Juliet laughed. "No, we probably wouldn't understand anyway."

Mary was watching from outside waiting for them to move with engine running she placed a hand against the motorhome and the door opened. "Is there a problem?"

The computer spoke, "no, Mary I'm just waiting for instructions you obviously didn't tell them about me."

"No, Freddie I forgot I must be getting old," she smiled.

James and Juliet looked at Mary saying together. "Freddie?"

"Yes, Freddie was my favourite dog so I named the computer Freddie."

"James and Juliet burst out laughing James asked, "Can Freddie really drive?"

Mary commented "just leave everything to Freddie, at least my motorhome won't be bent if he drives."

The door closed; James and Juliet just sat back and watched Freddie drive the motorhome. James and Juliet were not comfortable with the thought of a computer driving the motorhome to start with, although as the miles passed by they began to relax. Freddie spoke, "James, Juliet you might as well retire no one can see you're not at the wheel driving, just make yourselves comfortable and enjoy the journey we have over 250 miles to go before we arrived at the campsite which I've booked in advance."

James and Juliet moved to the rear of the motorhome and watched a large double bed lower from the side of the vehicle. Freddie spoke. "Don't worry I'm not watching."

They lay on the bed James turned to Juliet and passionately kissed her on the lips and placed his hand gently on her covered breast. She grabbed his hand, "no, James no." James reluctantly rolled onto his back. They hadn't made love since Fiona was born and James was becoming very frustrated with Juliet's lack of interest in him. It almost seemed they were just work colleagues instead of a married couple in love. Juliet rolled over to face James, "just give me a little time James please I don't want to get pregnant again."

"I thought you were on the pill Juliet?"

"I am, oh I don't know what's wrong with me," she professed earnestly.

James sighed and turned his back on Juliet. She lay on her back looking at the ceiling with tear filled eyes she knew she loved him so much and couldn't understand why she didn't want to make love with him. Was she really scared of becoming pregnant again or was there another reason? Juliet rose to her feet and walked to the front of the motorhome and phoned Margaret James's mother.

"Hi Margaret it's me Juliet can we talk?"

"What's wrong love?" Margaret enquired concerned at the sound of Juliet's voice.

"I can't bring myself to make love, oh damn this is so embarrassing I feel stupid."

Margaret responded firmly, "Is James trying to pressurise you, put him on the phone."

"No, Margaret it's not him, it's me I'm just not interested and I don't know why?"

Margaret laughed. "Don't worry my love it's quite normal I made James's father wait six months before I was interested."

"Thanks Margaret, at least I know I'm not weird, bye."

Freddie spoke, "That is not out of the ordinary, each female is affected differently after giving birth."

"Who the bloody hell asked you to interfere? Keep your nose out Freddie or I'll put a bullet in your circuits and give you something to worry about."

Freddie didn't respond.

They finally entered the campsite and Juliet quickly sat in the driving seat as the camp warden showed them where to park; they were going to stay there for three nights. James joined Juliet at the front of the motorhome, gazing out to the shoreline, seeing oil tankers and freighters anchored offshore, wondering whether one of these vessels would be carrying the explosives. Juliet moved to the back of the motorhome; pressing the button allowing her workstation to assemble. She used the high-powered surveillance equipment to scan the offshore ships. Freddie spoke, "I detect no explosives on any of the vessels Juliet I suggest you both take a stroll along the coastline and enjoy the fresh air after all you are supposed to be on holiday."

"Yes, Freddie you're right," James said with a deflated voice.

Juliet and James left the motorhome and casually walked along the shoreline Juliet reached for James's hand he glanced to her with a glimmer of a smile. She was trying her very best to reassure James all was well with their relationship and trying to focus on their mission at the same time. James could see the dust drifting from the quarry a little way ahead and the vapours rising from the chimney as the limestone was processed into cement. James released Juliet's hand and placed his arm around her waist and she responded likewise both occasionally glancing to each other.

Juliet suggested, "Let's sit for a while we're out of the wind here and it's quite secluded, we can watch the ships from here." They both seated themselves on the soft sand between the rocks. Juliet suddenly had feelings she hadn't felt for a long time and started to undo the buttons on her blouse, hoping James would take the initiative. James rested his back against the rock and didn't make any advances towards Juliet. She opened her blouse slightly professing she was warm as the reason for doing so. James just continued to look out to sea and ignore Juliet. Juliet, becoming very annoyed and frustrated, uncoupled her bra from the front and opened her blouse fully, grabbing James's hand and placing it on her breast. James immediately removed it, "I have a headache woman leave me alone," he smiled.

Before Juliet could respond James had moved towards her uncoupling her jeans and removing them along with her pants, within seconds they were making love the way they always did with great passion and tenderness. They finally dressed trying to remove as much sand as possible from the most inconvenient parts of their clothing. Juliet passionately kissed James; relieved she had finally made love again to the man she loved so much. They slowly walked back to the motorhome and both showered together. Juliet removed her dressing gown and slid into bed. James followed suit and before long they were making love again. Juliet's mind flooded with memories of the special moments James and her had spent together she felt a passion like she'd never felt before wanting to keep James in bed with her for as long as possible.

Mary's voice could be heard. "Stop eating James Juliet, you're supposed to be working." Mary chuckled, "I have more information; I thought we had disposed of Kahn's relations and organisation. Obviously not; if you'd been listening Juliet to the chatter," Mary emphasised continuing, "you would both realise a freighter is heading your way."

Juliet and James dressed quickly. "Sorry Mary," James professed continuing, "is Fiona all right?"

"Of course, she is with me and asleep."

Juliet moved to her workstation quickly, seeing a flash on the screen indicating the ship carrying the explosives. James also surveyed the information.

Mary instructed. "We estimate it will be 10 days before the cargo ship arrives, for some unknown reason it's moving very slowly. I want you to eliminate whoever is waiting for the ship's arrival then we can blow the vessel up out at sea. We suspect at least 10 terrorists involved onshore. James, Juliet, shoot to kill these are your instructions." Before James or Juliet could ask any questions Mary had broken contact. Freddie spoke. "Mary asked me to explain her sudden disappearance apparently Fiona was crying." James and Juliet burst out laughing at the thought of a young child controlling Mary when any adult who tried the same trick would either be shot or beaten to death.

Chapter 20

Next Destination

Freddie took control of the motorhome as they continued their journey north to Nairn a place they had visited previously on their honeymoon, only this time it was pure business. They travelled the 208 miles at a steady 50 miles an hour not wishing to attract attention by being captured on the variable speed cameras, finally pulling into a campsite 5 miles away from the town. After parking, Freddie jacked the motorhome up and the brand-new Lamborghini slid from underneath the belly of the vehicle. Juliet immediately jumped into the car with excitement much to her annoyance the car automatically started and manoeuvred itself away from the motorhome and parked alongside and the engine switched itself off. Juliet banged the steering wheel with frustration. Freddie spoke, "I also control the car, let me explain my options; I can shoot from the front and rear, you have bullet-proof glass and although the body looks fibreglass it is actually carbon fibre made to a top secret formula which is bullet-proof; my tyres are bullet-proof as well. Before you ask, you don't have an ejector seat. One added bonus; if anyone manages to break into the car I can electrify the steering wheel and they will be toast."

Juliet climbed out of the car not saying a word and returned to James in the motorhome complaining. "That's going to be a bundle of fun, Freddie controls the bloody car."

James laughed. "I suspected as much, if you remember what happened to the last car we had up here."

Juliet smiled kissing James on the lips.

The following morning, they both climbed in the Lamborghini; Freddie took control much to Juliet's annoyance and drove them to Fort George which was part Museum and barracks open to the public. The camp commander greeted them both, fully aware of their mission and assured them both if they needed any support his men would be made available. James and Juliet continued walking around the fort looking for any signs that may give them a clue to the whereabouts of the terrorists. James guided Juliet up onto the battlements where the old cannons sat slowly decaying from years of weathering.

James spotted an odd couple who didn't seem to be really interested in their surroundings but appeared to be waiting for someone. Juliet noted four Asian men approaching the couple; one man, was obviously dressed as a woman. The suspected terrorists gathered together occasionally looking over their shoulder to see if they were being observed. James quickly photographed the group and then held Juliet's hand making their way from the battlements towards the group. James then realised he recognised one of the men. Kahn's old chauffeur he steered Juliet away from the group. She looked at him rather puzzled until they went around the corner out of sight then James explained he recognised one of them. The photographs James had taken were immediately transmitted to headquarters where Mary carried out facial recognition.

Juliet and James observed the men from a concealed position and received a text message from Mary instructing them not to intervene, and to follow the group if possible. James and Juliet immediately left the fort, getting into the Lamborghini. Freddie spoke, "The car they arrived in is a blue Ford Orion over there, place a tracker on the car James and we can follow at a discreet distance."

James casually walked past the car pretending to drop something on the ground and placed a tracker under the wheel arch and quickly returned to the Lamborghini. Freddie confirmed the tracker was working and they drove off to a nearby village, parking up and waiting for the Orion to pass. Within half an hour the terrorists were on the move; James and Juliet could clearly see on Freddie's display that the car was approaching and passed with five people in the car, which meant one had stayed behind and was obviously leaving in another vehicle or on a coach. Freddie started to follow while James and Juliet checked their firearms.

James commented, "It is bloody strange having a car that drives itself Juliet don't you think?"

Not Guilty

Before Juliet could respond Freddie spoke, "the car is not driving it-self I am driving."

"Who's got his knickers in a twist now then," Juliet joked.

Freddie didn't respond James smiled at Juliet's comment. They'd been travelling for some distance over 50 miles and suddenly the terrorists had pulled over and stopped. Freddie was gaining on them very quickly. Freddie pulled over into a layby displaying a detailed aerial survey of the area which showed a small property 50 yards further up the road. Mary's voice could be heard. "James, Juliet, eliminate the terrorists and anyone else who's in the house."

James and Juliet left the vehicle and cut across through the woodland until they were within yards of the house. James whispered, "Can you see them slapping a woman she can't be anything to do with them?"

Juliet replied quietly, "let's not shoot her until we find out what's going on, we'll just take out the other five, I'll go round the back in case any of them try to escape you take them out through the window if you can."

Juliet kissed James on the lips and moved off towards the back of the house. James positioned himself against the wall. Then like a coiled spring he broke the pain of glass shooting three of the terrorists in the head he heard two more shots. He ran to the rear of the property to see Juliet standing over two bodies. They both ran in the house to find a young woman on the floor gagged and bound. James quickly eased the woman to her feet and down into a chair. Juliet removed her knife and cut away the bondage from her hands and feet. James removed the tape gently from her mouth trying to ease the tape from her blonde hair without inflicting any further pain.

"Thank you both," the young woman said, "my name is Natasha and you are James and Juliet."

James and Juliet looked at each other shocked. "How do you know who we are?" James asked quickly.

"I'm also an agent we know all about you."

"You're KGB? You certainly speak with a Russian accent," Juliet enquired.

"No, we specialise in terrorists and their elimination just like you two you could almost say were on the same team with the same goals."

Natasha rose to her feet moving to the sink and washing her face, her long blonde hair cascaded down her spine. Juliet glanced to James monitoring his expression to see if he was showing any signs of interest in Natasha.

Juliet contacted Mary and explained the situation to her. Mary instructed Juliet to pass her phone to Natasha which she did immediately. Natasha and Mary were speaking in Russian to each other neither James nor Juliet could understand the conversation, they appeared to be laughing and joking on the phone. Finally Natasha passed the mobile back to Juliet.

"I will take their car," Natasha said continuing, "I must wait for further instructions Mary will contact her counterpart and inform them I'm safe as if they would really care," she commented. James suggested, "Let Juliet drive you to your destination you look as if you could do with the rest."

"I'll be fine," she smiled kissing James on the cheek, "you are lucky Juliet to have a man like this one he would die to protect you." Juliet folded her arms wondering whether James enjoyed the attention of Natasha who had a gorgeous figure and beautiful complexion although showing a few bruises from where she'd been punched. They all went their separate ways, James and Juliet returned to the motorhome. Juliet sat very quietly on the settee looking out of the window. James made them both a coffee and joined her on the settee placing his arm around her shoulder "What's the matter Juliet is it because Natasha kissed me on the cheek?" Juliet turned to face him. "I wish I'd of shot her that was our instructions." She said firmly.

"Woe, woe where's that coming from Juliet it's not like you? Blimey she only kissed me on the cheek it meant nothing at all you're my girl."

"I bet you'd go to bed with her if you had the chance James I saw the look on your face." Before James could respond Mary intervened.

"Juliet you are being bloody ridiculous you are obviously not fit for duty I'm sending you home. I cannot afford to have the mission wrecked by your jealousy which is totally unfounded. James is not like that Juliet and if you don't know by now you never will you silly woman. "

"I'm not going home there's nothing wrong with me and you shouldn't bloody listen to private conversations," Juliet protested.

"One more outburst Juliet and you're out of here do you get the message," Mary enforced with authority.

"Okay, I get the message sorry Mary."

Mary ordered Juliet to stay in the motorhome and monitor the situation from her workstation. James would be assisted by another agent yet to be decided. Juliet knew there was no point in protesting, she'd already put her foot in it and she certainly didn't want to be sent home away from James.

Not Guilty

At least she would know his every movement by his implant so whatever he did she would know about it.

Mary advised, "we must find the one missing terrorist who you recognised at Fort George James and eliminate him."

"No problem Mary, just tell me where he is and I'll shoot him."

We know he's somewhere in the area probably in town you will have to search discreetly James. The new male agent will meet you in the car park by the beach."

Juliet smiled with relief after hearing Mary's comments. James checked his gun and went out and jumped into the Lamborghini. Freddie drove the vehicle. Mary came over the intercom.

"James you are meeting up with Natasha."

The smile vanished from James's face, "I know you don't like deception but I couldn't risk Juliet becoming jealous again, the mission is important James you must realise that Juliet will not be able to track Natasha she will never know she's in the car and Freddie will say nothing"

"I'm not happy Mary but I do understand your reasoning so I'll play along for now."

Freddie parked the car in the beach car park. James got out and sat on the bench looking out to sea he almost thought he should phone Juliet and tell her the truth. He knew she would only blow a fuse and probably shoot him when he returned to the motorhome, regardless whether he was guilty of anything or not. Natasha sat on the seat beside him James didn't realise it was her to start with. She was wearing a flowered short dress with very few buttons actually fastened on the front leaving nothing for the imagination he could plainly see her bra and the top of her breasts.

"We meet again James," she smiled flicking her long blonde hair over her shoulder.

"You're not really dressed for combat Natasha more like seduction."

"I am playing the part of your wife and we are on holiday together so we can stroll around the town and no one will think any the wiser." She smiled continuing, "I am sorry if you find me attractive, surely you wouldn't want to walk around town with an old bag," she laughed. Kissing him on the cheek and then on the lips which he tried not to respond to without much success. Natasha rubbed his leg, "come on we'll have a coffee in the cafe over there it's such a nice day and for once I'm with a handsome man."

"If you were my wife Natasha, you would be across my knee by now, displaying yourself the way you are you're almost like a tart." James watched the smile drain from her face and she buttoned her dress covering her breasts completely.

"Are you happy now husband?" She asked linking her arm in his as they walked towards the coffee shop.

James couldn't help himself he burst into laughter and so did Natasha. She commented "Is what you say you don't want my goods on display they are only for private viewing?" James could not stop laughing at her comment.

They finished their coffee and slowly walked into town. Natasha complained, "These high heel shoes are ridiculous they hurt my feet." James grabbed her hand pulling her into a shoe shop. "Pick something that is more comfortable and throw those ridiculous shoes in the bin." Natasha selected a more comfortable shoe and did exactly as James had suggested and threw the others in the bin. James paid for the new shoes on his credit card. Natasha's smile broadly once again linking her arm in his then turned to face him in the street and kissed him passionately on the lips he tried to ease her way but for some unknown reason couldn't find the strength or he just didn't want to. "Now I see why Juliet loves you so much, you are kind and generous just as it states in your file."

"What else does it say in your file about me?" He asked eagerly.

"Only you are a cold-blooded killer and the most dangerous agent they possess."

"I know absolutely nothing about you Natasha I didn't know you existed until a few hours ago"

"I am of no importance, my agency would not care if you put a bullet in my head or anyone else for that matter, we are disposable in their eyes."

"I'm glad I don't work for your outfit," he smiled.

They entered a dark alleyway and before their eyes could become accustomed to the darkness, James heard someone approaching from behind he turned quickly; seeing the reflection of a knife, within seconds he had broken the man's neck who lay on the ground motionless. James grabbed Natasha's hand, hurrying out into the daylight and away from the scene so they could not be linked to the death. They continued walking quickly to the Lamborghini the doors automatically opened and they climbed in. "Ha, this is Freddie your car."

"Hello Natasha," Freddie responded.

"Is there anything you don't know about our organisation Natasha," James asked.

"No, I don't think so, you have your spies we have ours, you listen to our communications we listen to yours, it's ridiculous considering we're on the same mission."

"Are you married Natasha?"

"No, it's not permitted in our organisation and it didn't used to be in yours, although they have made an exception in your case."

"There is nothing in the regulations saying you can't take me to bed James, which I would rather like you to do," Natasha offered smiling.

"James stared at Natasha after hearing her comment he was surprised by her forwardness."

"I would never dream of betraying my wife's trust," he said firmly.

"I think you are telling me porkies James, what about when you were married to Jackie? What did you do to the two women you were sent to assassinate."

"Is there nothing about me you don't know," he protested.

"No, there is nothing in your life I don't know about, that is why I volunteered to work with you and of course, with Mary's approval."

Mary's voice came over the intercom. "Natasha stop trying to get my agent into bed with you please, you won't succeed with James he would sooner kill you than betray his wife so bear that in mind."

"Don't be such a spoilsport Mary, he's already killed someone to protect me, he must care something for me and he does kiss really nice." she teased.

James felt his face turn red with embarrassment listening to the two of them.

"Don't worry James Juliet's computer is being fed false information so she's perfectly happy. She has no idea what's going on in the interests of interagency co-operation. Please don't shoot their agent."

They laughed. Mary knew if Natasha got on the wrong side of James she would be in a body bag and he wouldn't think twice about it.

James and Natasha left the Lamborghini next to a retirement home giving the impression they were visiting relatives and continued walking on into town, hoping to see signs of the missing terrorist. Natasha continually held James's hand as they walked the streets occasionally stopping and looking in shop windows to ensure everyone had the allusion of holidaymakers.

James spotted the terrorist walking into an alleyway. James ran after him and returned a few minutes later wiping the blood off his hands on his handkerchief. Natasha was shocked by the swiftness of James's actions.

"You have dispatched the man?" James nodded holding Natasha's hand and they continued walking as if nothing had happened and returned to the Lamborghini. Freddie opened the doors as they approached and they climbed in. "Contact Mary Freddie, inform her, the terrorist has been eliminated and we are moving on to our next destination in the morning."

Mary spoke over the intercom, "well done you two, excellent job."

Natasha spoke, "It was nothing to do with me Mary, before I could blink James disposed of him he's so quick and efficient."

"That's my boy," Mary replied continuing, "yes, move onto the next destination in the morning and because this operation has been such a success, I will arrange for Natasha to join you there without Juliet knowing."

"You're playing with fire Mary," James warned.

"Don't I always James," She replied firmly.

"I think we should be honest," Natasha said calmly, "It is unfair on Juliet and James I will talk to her myself and explained the situation, if you will not Mary."

"You will do as you're told Natasha, you are under my jurisdiction," Mary shouted fearing the consequences.

"I am not one of your puppets, I do as I please you do not frighten me Mary."

Mary sighed. James commented, "Honesty is the best policy Mary, I have to agree with Natasha if Juliet ever found out my marriage would be over at least if she knows upfront we cannot be accused of deception, I'll just have to face the consequences if there are any."

"Be it on your own heads," Mary concluded.

James instructed, "Freddie, take us to the motorhome."

The Lamborghini started to move the 5 miles seem to disappear in seconds. Juliet came from the motorhome watching the doors lift on the Lamborghini and Natasha stepped out one side and James the other. Juliet turned and went back inside. Natasha followed her and James a few moments later. "I suppose you've been fucking my husband?" Juliet shouted. Before Natasha could reply Juliet walked over to James and slapped his face very hard seeing lipstick on his cheek. "I trusted you James and you cheated on me after all we've been through together." James didn't move;

Not Guilty

Juliet went to strike him again and he didn't try to defend himself. Natasha grabbed her wrist.

"Don't strike him, he isn't guilty of anything I offered to go to bed with him and he refused so if you want to try and hit somebody try me." Natasha said calmly, continuing, "Of course I kissed him, I was playing the part of his wife while we searched and found the missing terrorist, James disposed of him. Now calm down you're being irrational Juliet, you know what our business is like sometimes it's totally crap the things we have to do to succeed."

Natasha released Juliet's wrist and went to make some coffee. "Juliet flung her arms around James's neck gently kissing him, "I'm sorry James I should have known you wouldn't cheat on me for any reason I'm just a silly bitch."

Mary's voice could be heard, "that went better than I thought, you're not a silly bitch Juliet your hormones are not settled yet, you're not thinking clearly and I should never have let you come on this mission, it's my fault. If I'd known Natasha was available your presence would not have been necessary."

James sat quietly on the settee letting Natasha and Juliet talk amongst themselves, his face was stinging from the impact of Juliet's hand and the force she used, he was just glad she hadn't decided to shoot him. Mary suggested, "Juliet, Natasha if you're very quick you can go shopping so Natasha has a new change of clothes." They immediately left and drove off towards town.

Mary spoke to James over the intercom. "What is your opinion of Natasha James? Do you think she would make a good agent if she was permanently posted here with us?"

"I don't know her well enough Mary to make a decision, she doesn't seem very quick on her feet. I had to dispatch the last two people we came across one was trying to stab her in the back."

"Natasha's instructions were from me, not to interfere, to let you dispose of the targets, she was just to observe and play the part of your wife, which she did extremely well I thought although I must agree with you, she was giving you too much to look at and it could have been a distraction," Mary laughed.

"It's your decision Mary if I was you I'd see how the rest of this mission plays out before you make a final assessment."

"My main concern James is can we trust her after all she is from the other side?"

"I will shoot her if I suspect her of anything," James said calmly.

"Thank you James you are the one person in the organisation I can rely on to do what is right."

Chapter 21
Seek and Destroy

They arrived at Poolewe after a short journey of 86 miles. Natasha travelled with them in the motorhome. It was extremely difficult to navigate around the site with such a large vehicle. Freddie removed the Lamborghini from under the motorhome's belly, much to everyone's amazement on the campsite and after seeing Natasha and Juliet leave the motorhome closely followed by James, tongues started wagging. One man and two beautiful women seem to be every man's dream. James thought it would be amusing if he walked between the two young women and placed his arm around their waist. James whispered to them both, "let's give them something to talk about," he chuckled.

Juliet kissed James on the cheek and so did Natasha knowing full well they were being watched by other campers. They strolled out of the campsite looking at the surrounding scenery and across Loch Ewe. They slowly returned to the motorhome trying to dodge the midges that appeared to be making a meal of everyone on site. Freddie spoke as they boarded. "I will eliminate the infestation."

The door closed and Freddie released a chemical into the air which disposed of the on-board midges. Natasha removed her blouse and so did Juliet brushing each other down and inspecting for midges.

Natasha's said releasing her bra "They get everywhere horrible little bloody bugs."

James expected Juliet to throw a tantrum after Natasha had removed her bra and was standing in view of him. Much to James's surprise Juliet did exactly the same. He watched them both inspecting the inside of their bras carrying on as if he didn't exist.

Natasha went into the shower first closely followed by Juliet. He could hear them talking as if they'd been lifetime buddies, which in some respects was a relief to James. He couldn't imagine Juliet ever allowing him to see Natasha topless in her presence. Perhaps he concluded Juliet's hormones have finally settled down and she realised she would never lose her husband to Natasha whatever she did to encourage him. Juliet and Natasha dressed in jeans and blouses.

Natasha announced, "Were going for a drive, we have a hunch where the explosives could be landing, at the old, Russian anchorage point just along the coast."

Juliet kissed James, Natasha smiled patting his cheek and climbed into the Lamborghini and drove off. James sat at the workstation monitoring their progress. Mary's image appeared on the screen." They seem to be getting on extremely well James which I find rather odd. Juliet is fully aware Natasha has feelings for you."

James thought for a moment, "You don't think Natasha would try and eliminate Juliet Mary?"

"No, Natasha really wants to stay in the country and work alongside us; it would be detrimental to her cause if she was found to be involved in Juliet's demise."

Juliet and Natasha travelled along the single track road until they reached the far end and started searching the derelict base most of which has started to crumble from years of deterioration since the Second World War. Suddenly without warning a piece of concrete gave way from the ceiling striking Juliet on the head and shoulder she fell to the floor. Natasha tried to contact her using the two-way radio. Natasha drew her gun and frantically searched the derelict buildings finally coming across Juliet. She struggled to move the rubble and to carry Juliet back to the car. Natasha instructed Freddie to contact Mary and arrange for a helicopter to meet them on the nearby beach where it was safe for the helicopter to land. Juliet was bleeding heavily from a wound on her forehead. Natasha did her best to stem the bleeding while she waited patiently for the helicopter, finally it arrived the paramedics took Juliet and flew off. Natasha returned to the campsite entering the motorhome in haste as her blouse was covered in blood.

James stared in horror. "What's happened, where's Juliet?" Natasha explained the chain of events that took place. James poured her a large whiskey and seated himself by her, placing is arm around her shoulder and gently kissing her on the forehead. "Thank you Natasha for helping Juliet."

"She would have done the same for me James we are like sisters," Natasha remarked wiping a tear from her eye.

Mary's voice came over the intercom. "James, Juliet is being flown to London she has a serious head wound and a dislocated shoulder I will keep you posted I know you want to be with her but it is essential you complete the mission."

"I understand Mary," James sighed. "Take care of her Mary and keep me posted."

"I certainly will James don't worry, she will have the best care possible."

Natasha placed her drink on the table and started to unbutton her bloodstained blouse walking to the wardrobe and removing a clean one. Then realised the blood had gone through onto her bra which she then removed and discarded and just slipped the blouse on and buttoned. She returned and sat by James resting her head on his shoulder. They sat there quietly for a while neither saying a word. Natasha then stood up and walked over to the side of the bed where she removed all her clothes and went into the shower. James was blaming himself; he should have gone and checked the area out, then Juliet wouldn't have been in danger. Natasha dried herself and slipped on a dressing gown returning to the settee after switching the kettle on to make a coffee. They finished their refreshments and stood looking at each other wondering whether to embrace and if they did what would be the outcome?

James slid into bed and Natasha joined him after removing her dressing gown. "We can sleep together James without anything happening." Natasha commented.

"Yes, we are adults and professionals."

Natasha rested her head on James's chest and placed her arm across his stomach. James made no advancement towards Natasha he was determined to control his emotions although she was a beautiful woman.

Natasha had woken early showered and started making breakfast for them both. James stirred to see Natasha laying the table and pouring the coffee. They smiled at each other both knowing if circumstances were different they would still be in bed together making love. James immediately reached for his mobile and phoned Mary to ascertain Juliet's condition. Mary confirmed Juliet was still unconscious but stable and the doctors thought she would make a full recovery once the swelling had gone down in her brain.

James dressed quickly sitting at the table by Natasha who had taken one of his T-shirts from the wardrobe and slipped it on while she made breakfast leaving nothing to the imagination she hadn't even bothered to put pants on. She was performing as if she was married to him or at the very least a lover.

Natasha finished her breakfast along with James. She commented. "I wish you had made love to me last night I would not have stopped you."

James replied sipping his coffee, "I feel awfully guilty Natasha. God knows how we didn't end up making love the way we feel about each other and we shouldn't, we are professionals."

Natasha draped her arms around his shoulders and kissed him passionately on the lips pressing her covered breasts against his chest. James commented, "Please don't Natasha, I would find it easier to kill you than to sleep with you and that's a terrible thing to say."

"I don't think you'd kill me James unless I betrayed you or the organisation," she smiled, removing the T-shirt and kissing him again on the lips and neck.

James gently eased her away from him. "Natasha stop it, I'm married and yes I am attracted to you but I can't"…..

Mary had been monitoring the conversation and watching Natasha's behaviour from a surveillance camera, instructed Freddie to blast her with a jet of cold water from the sprinkler system inside the motorhome. Natasha "screamed." Moving away from James immediately. Mary spoke over the intercom, "Natasha behave and stop tormenting James he needs to have a clear mind." James we have been monitoring a range Rover carrying four terrorists driving up the A 82 they are cutting across to your location obviously heading towards the Old Russian anchorage. Freddie has the registration of the vehicle programmed into the Lamborghini I want you and Natasha to destroy the range Rover take no prisoners do you understand me James?"

"Loud and clear Mary," James replied glancing across to Natasha.

"Yes Mary."

Natasha sprayed herself trying to prevent the midges from having a meal at her expense. James did likewise and they left the campsite in the Lamborghini Freddie was driving as usual. James and Natasha monitored

Not Guilty

the display watching the range Rover. Much to their surprise the terrorists didn't head for the old anchorage they changed direction, taking the Ullapool road which went past the refuelling point for the Navy. Freddie gave chase, the range Rover was travelling at very high speed as if they knew they were being followed. James instructed Freddie to shoot the nearside rear tyre and fuel tank once they had reached the high point on the cliff road where there were no barriers to stop vehicles going off.

Freddie announced, "I have a malfunction my guns are jammed."

"Ram the bloody vehicle pushed it off the road Freddie"

"Freddie responded quickly, "I am not permitted to commit suicide."

"Give me control of the bloody vehicle that is an order Freddie."

"James, don't be so stupid you'll kill us both," Natasha voiced holding her seatbelt.

James took control of the Lamborghini pushing his foot to the floor the car roared into life closing on the range Rover in seconds, he could see one of the terrorists looking out of the back window holding a machine-gun. The terrorist started to fire, glass shattered on the range Rover although the bullets just bounced off the Lamborghini's windscreen. Natasha closed her eyes fearing the worst. James rammed the range Rover on the bend taking them both over the cliff. Freddie activated the foam dispensers engulfing the occupants. Both vehicles rolled down the cliff face and entered the cold water. James broke the foam away from his face which seemed more like polystyrene stopping you from being injured. James broke the polystyrene away from Natasha's face. Water was starting to leak into the car as they sank. Freddie spoke, "I have informed Mary of what has taken place she will arrange for the Lamborghini to be salvaged."

"What about us?" James asked.

"I can't repeat what she said when I told her you had wrecked the Lamborghini."

"Once the car has filled with water James I will release the doors and you and Natasha can swim to the surface."

Natasha glanced across to James, "you are a crazy man James you could have killed us both."

James smiled, "Not today Natasha, I hope you can swim," he joked.

"This isn't funny James Natasha complained we could have been killed are all British agents as stupid as you?"

Finally, the car filled with water sufficiently for Freddie to release the doors. James and Natasha swam to the surface, searching for any terrorists that may have survived from the range Rover. James dived searching for the range Rover in the murky water finally coming across the remains of the vehicle and seeing the occupants still inside which made him smile. James swam ashore to find Natasha sat on a rock shivering.

"We'll not be able to climb up there Natasha it's too steep it looks like we'll have to swim." He said placing is arm around Natasha trying to warm her with a cuddle.

James could see a speedboat approaching in the distance he stood up and waved as it became closer, he could see it was from the Royal Navy. Mary had obviously sent a craft to find them and take them back to shore, where they could return to the motorhome. A sailor helped them aboard giving them each a blanket to keep warm. A car awaited them on landing to transport Natasha and James back to the motorhome. James and Natasha changed quickly into dry clothes. The workstation automatically came out and Mary appeared on the screen.

"Well James you've done it again managed to destroy government property." She then smiled, "well done, I'm proud of you and I'm pleased neither of you are hurt."

Natasha spoke, "This man is crazy he should be locked up."

Mary laughed. "No, he is just a dedicated agent who has the ability to get the job done regardless of the consequences." Mary continued, "I have some good news; Juliet has regained consciousness and she is fine, no permanent damage, her scans show she is the same as she's always been. She should be able to return home within a fortnight and she asked me to thank Natasha for saving her."

"My pleasure," Natasha voiced, "and I hope she gets well quickly."

James kissed Natasha on the cheek.

"James," Mary said changing the tone of her voice to one of business. "The mission is still not finished, the freighter will be in your area within the next two days. If there are any more terrorists out there waiting for the ship, we want you to deal with them James."

"My pleasure Mary," he smiled.

"I've arranged for a replacement car to be delivered to you within the next six hours in the meantime you two relax and prepare yourself for what lays ahead."

"Will do boss."

Mary laughed and the screen went blank.

"What would you like to do Natasha?" James asked.

"I would like you to take me to bed, I know that's not going to happen."

"And your second choice," James laughed.

"Take me out shopping, we can go to Ullapool" ....

Freddie interrupted and I'm driving if you're taking the motorhome." Natasha and James both burst into laughter at Freddie's comment.

James went and spoke to the camp warden and explained their Lamborghini had broken down and they were taking the motorhome off site and would be back later, so keep their space free.

Freddie, the extremely skilled computer, drove the motorhome from the campsite and headed for their destination. Natasha changed into her flowered dress which was very short with an extremely low neck line making sure all her attributes were fully visible. James commented, "Natasha you are a beautiful woman why do you dress like that?"

"If you don't want me James, I will have to find someone who does."

James sighed wondering why he should care how Natasha presented herself, he was happily married with children.

They arrived at their destination and Freddie parked the motorhome near to a clifftop viewing point. James and Natasha strolled along the coastline holding hands; it appeared to be deserted. Without giving a further thought to the consequences of his actions, he scooped Natasha up in his arms and kissed her passionately laying her down in the tallgrass, removing her pants and started making love to her, she did not resist in the slightest, it was something she had wanted for a long time. He caressed her firm breasts becoming intertwined in passionate love making. James finally rolled onto his back in the grass. Natasha rolled towards him and continued to kiss his neck and lips. Within a short while they were making love again and finally they tidied themselves and headed for the town centre. Natasha smiled broadly, she had achieved her goal of encouraging James to make love to her. James was feeling as guilty as hell and knew he would have to tell Juliet the truth regardless of the consequences.

"I will say nothing to Juliet James I promise you I just wanted you so desperately," Natasha reassured.

James sighed heavily kissing Natasha on the cheek. "I will have to tell her the truth Natasha I just couldn't resist you any longer."

"Don't be a fool James as much as I want you for myself, don't destroy your marriage."

"She will know Natasha, Juliet isn't a fool. If I was your husband you'd know if I was sleeping with somebody else?"

Natasha looked to the floor "I suppose you are correct James; women seem to have a second sense." Natasha continued, "it's my fault, let me explain what happened to Juliet I will say I got you drunk and raped you."

James laughed, "I don't drink, well not much anyway."

Natasha grinned holding onto James's arm leaning her head against his shoulder. James and Natasha entered a restaurant had a meal and spent the rest of the day kissing and cuddling like newlyweds enjoying the evening breeze. They slowly made their way back to the motorhome. When suddenly Natasha dropped to the floor like a stone lifeless, James could see blood running from her head she'd been shot but from where.

Freddie scanned the area with his infrared cameras. There was a thud against the motorhome as another shot had been fired aimed at James obviously missing the target. James quickly carried Natasha's lifeless body inside the motorhome. The tears stream down his face. He shouted, "Freddie where are they?"

"Two miles away within my firing range on the edge of woodland."

"Get going Freddie come on I want to kill the bastards."

"Allow me James to execute the assassin it will be quicker than trying to drive there."

"Go on Freddie take him out and anyone else who's with him."

James watched the monitor while Freddie lined up the shot and saw the assassin drop on the floor another man appeared from behind a tree. Freddie shot him regardless whether he was involved or not. "Well done Freddie take me to them I want to see if there's any ID on either of them."

Freddie didn't hesitate. James didn't realise how fast the motorhome of this size could travel Freddie was not sparing the horses he was on a mission just like James. Freddie told James he had notified Mary and she was sending a helicopter to collect Natasha's body to be returned to Russia and be buried by her parents. Freddie parked the motorhome on the grass verge. James made sure his gun was loaded and entered the wood coming across the two male bodies, both of Asian descent. He photographed what was left of their faces after Freddie had shot them and sent the images to Mary. He searched their clothing for ID but they were carrying nothing, all that was left on the ground a high-powered rifle. James carefully picked it up returning to the motorhome. He then kissed Natasha on her lifeless lips and wrapped her in a bed sheet. Within a little while a helicopter had landed and Natasha's body was taken away.

Mary's face appeared on the monitor she could see the state James was in. "I know this is no comfort when you lose a colleague but it goes with the territory son."

James nodded "I know Mary but it still bloody hurts."

"Just remember James you made her very happy woman before she left this world."

"How do you know?"

"The chip planted in you went off the scale it monitors your heartbeat and blood pressure."

"Oh," James replied, "I suppose you think I'm a right bastard?"

"No, James I don't know how you resisted her for so long, I shan't say anything to Juliet, let the incident drift into history where it belongs."

"There's blood everywhere Mary the motorhome looks a mess."

"Don't worry James. Freddie will deal with the problem."

James watched the stains vanish before his eyes as if nothing had taken place.

"Your new car will arrive within the next hour. Go back to the campsite I'm instructing the agent to stay with you as backup until we are sure we have dealt with this threat completely. I'm instructing the air force to blow the ship out of the water. But I'd like you to spend a few more days up there, try and relax if you can."

"Okay Mary just as you wish."

Chapter 22
Double Vision

Freddie drove the motorhome slowly back to the campsite passing the bend where James had pushed the range Rover off the cliff. He saw a salvage vessel lifting the Lamborghini from the water and placing it on deck. He shook his head in disbelief and felt if he'd been paying more attention to the situation, Natasha may not have died. He felt he should have been aware of the threat to their lives considering they'd been killing terrorists in the area. It should have been obvious to him they would retaliate at the first opportunity.

Freddie parked the motorhome just as the new black Lamborghini entered the campsite. James left the motorhome to greet the new agent. He watched the door open he staggered backwards and fell against the motorhome. The woman delivering the Lamborghini was the spitting image of Natasha. James rubbed his eyes in disbelief then gathered his senses and greeted the agent who was wearing an all in one black leather outfit. She held her hand out. "Hi, James I'm Jasmine," continuing, "sorry to hear about Juliet and Natasha."

"Thank you," he smiled, "climb aboard."

They both went inside James made them both a coffee and they seated on the settee. James just couldn't believe the resemblance, he had to ask. "You weren't related to Natasha were you?"

Jasmine smiled. "No, it's just good fortunate I look like her. There were no plans for me to stay until what took place, then Mary thought no one would realise Natasha was missing if I was here. I will have to go and buy some clothes I only have the outfit I'm wearing."

James commented. "Have a look in the wardrobe Juliet clothes are in there and Natasha's it will tide you over until we go shopping."

"Thanks."

Mary appeared on the monitor. "Jasmine you've arrived. Good, do exactly as James instructs you Jasmine, he is the senior field agent and you have barely finished training so listen to what he tells you."

"Yes Mary." She replied nervously.

"I'm sorry James," Mary expressed, continuing. "It must have been a shock when you saw Jasmine you could barely tell Natasha and her apart."

"I understand Mary she is an obvious choice how much experience does she have in the field?"

"To be honest James none, she's only been a paper pusher and I thought if she was going to be a good agent she should learn from the best and that is you of course."

Jasmine turned bright red with embarrassment. James placed his arm around her shoulder reassuringly. "Don't worry Jasmine we all have to start somewhere and that includes me."

"Just enjoy yourselves." Mary advised, "Until I contact you again. Jasmine, remember what I said, listen to James."

"Yes, Mary I understand and thank you for giving me the opportunity."

Mary vanished from the monitor. Jasmine sipped her coffee nervously now James knew she was a rookie. James enquired. "Have you ever killed anybody?"

"Not yet, although I have completed the firearms training and I scored an average on the target practice." She smiled, "I'm sure I could kill someone if I have too." She said trying to reassure James.

"Let me see your gun Jasmine." Jasmine quickly removed her gun and handed over to James without question. James placed the gun against her head. She looked horrified although she didn't scream. "That's the first mistake you've made," James said firmly. "Never give your gun to anyone, how do you know I'm not a double agent?"

"Sorry I'm not very good am I?"

"I made the same mistake when I first started. It's a lesson you don't forget once you've been told, whoever wants your gun shoot first, then ask questions later," he smiled.

Jasmine smiled, "thank you I shan't forget." She continued. "I'd like to shower and change which clothes should I select if any of them fit me of course," she said standing up.

James went over to the wardrobe and opened the doors. "Help yourself Jasmine, I'll go for a walk and give you some privacy," he smiled.

"Thanks James."

James left the motorhome and walked across the road from the campsite to the shoreline sitting on a bench. His mobile rang Juliet.

"Hi love how you feeling?"

"I'm okay James, more to the point how you coping I heard what happened to Natasha she was really a nice person when you got to know her."

"Yes, I'm rather devastated I should have paid more attention to my surroundings."

You can't blame yourself James it could have been me"......

"Don't talk like that Juliet, I'm having enough trouble dealing with the loss now and to even consider it could have been you. Well it isn't worth thinking about."

"Another week and I can go home I can't wait to have you back with me and our lovely son and daughter."

"Okay, love you get some rest I'll be home soon, I love you. Bye."

James glanced to his watch guessing half an hour was long enough for Jasmine to shower and change. He slowly walked back to the motorhome and entered. Jasmine had changed into one of Natasha's dresses not leaving much to the imagination. He guessed he was just old-fashioned and would say nothing about her attire. Jasmine finished drying her hair and made a coffee for them both sitting beside James on the settee. She remarked, "Do I look okay?" The dress is a little tight around my boobs and a little shorter than I would normally where but it will have to do until we go shopping."

"I see what you mean," he smiled, "doesn't leave much to the imagination."

Jasmine blushed, "sorry I can't find anything else that fits me."

"We don't have much to eat in here I'll take you out to the local hotel this evening. I don't know where you'll holster your gun," he laughed looking at how tight the dress was.

Jasmine giggled and slapped him on the shoulder, "don't be rude."

"How old are you Jasmine? And what do your parents think of your chosen career?"

"I'm 19 not that you should ask a lady's age and I was brought up in an orphanage my parents didn't want me."

"Just like Juliet she was brought up in an orphanage for some of her life before she joined the agency what a coincidence."

James thought to himself he would make sure nothing happened to Jasmine she was his responsibility and he would give her the best training he could although he felt he was still learning himself. They sprayed each other with midge repellent and left the campsite in the Lamborghini as usual Freddie drove taking them the short distance to the hotel. They entered the restaurant and seating themselves by the window. They both settled for steak with all the trimmings and a bottle of wine. James was sitting opposite, struggling to keep his eyes off her bulging breasts trying to escape the tight dress. Jasmine commented, "You'll go blind James," smiling with satisfaction at his attention.

James joked, "I think they'll jump out and bite me in a minute."

Jasmine laughed, almost choking. "You're quite safe James as long as I don't breathe out," she smiled.

Jasmine made James feel relaxed and he was really starting to enjoy the evening. They finished the bottle of wine between them and headed for the door after paying the bill. They were sitting in the car chatting and laughing at the evening's events. Freddie interrupted their conversation. "James a car has just passed with a registration linked to a terrorist shall I follow?"

"Yes." James said firmly.

James checked his gun as Freddie drove the car. All the colour had drained from Jasmine's expression she was obviously terrified this was her first real mission. She fumbled with her purse she had borrowed removing her gun and checking the clip was full of bullets. Her hands were trembling and she dropped her purse to the floor then proceeded to rip the skirt between her legs to give her more freedom. James thought she had taken a sensible decision although she still looked petrified. Freddie spoke, "There are no cars coming in either direction shall I dispose of the vehicle?"

"No, Freddie, just take out the back tyre. I'd like a live one for a change if possible for interrogation."

Freddie shot the back tyre and the terrorist car and it came to a halt. James jumped out of the Lamborghini closely followed by Jasmine holding her gun with both hands shaking. Before the terrorist had chance to move

James pulled the door open and put the gun to his head. "Handcuff him Jasmine," James said pulling him from the car.

"Oh fuck, I didn't bring my handcuffs," Jasmine said aloud in frustration at her own inefficiency.

"Take mine from my jacket pocket," James instructed firmly.

She followed his instructions to the letter. "Follow me Jasmine in the Lamborghini I'll drive this one to a secluded location and we'll wait for Mary to send the helicopter to collect him."

James bundled the terrorist back into the red Citroen and drove off towards a secluded beach not far away, driving very carefully on the flat tyre. Within half an hour a military helicopter had landed and collected the terrorist from James. James searched the car and discovered in the boot a number of detonators and maps which he removed and placed in the Lamborghini behind his seat. "Freddie, move away from the Citroen and put a bullet in the petrol tank the police will think joyriders have torched the car."

Freddie did exactly as he'd been instructed the car burst into flames. Jasmine sat very quietly trembling from the experience. James patted her on the leg. "It's okay you've nothing to worry about."

"I forgot my handcuffs James you could have been in real trouble and I wasn't there to back you up."

"No worries, I'd have shot the bastard," he smiled. Jasmine laughed feeling relieved she wasn't going to be roasted for her stupidity.

Freddie drove them back to the motorhome. Jasmine flopped down on the settee trying to absorb all that had taken place. Mary appeared on the monitor, "I believe congratulations are in order James, you got me a live one. How did Jasmine perform? From what I can see she's wearing virtually nothing was that your idea James?" She asked frostily.

Before James could respond Jasmine spoke, "it wasn't James's fault the way I'm dressed, I don't have any clothes here and I had to make do with what was available so don't blame James."

"You already have an admirer and a fan club James," Mary chuckled. Continuing, "buy her some clothes tomorrow James I don't like my agents looking like tarts unless it's absolutely necessary."

"I was going to anyway Mary," he expressed firmly and the monitor went blank.

Not Guilty

Jasmine stood up and walked over close to the shower she slipped her dress off, pants and bra and entered the shower not concerned in the slightest James was still in the motorhome which rather surprised him. She came out a short while later just wrapping herself in a towel and drying her hair with another. She joined James on the settee in the meantime James had made them both a coffee. "Jasmine a few hours ago you were a shy reserved young girl, now you don't appear to give a damn?"

"Well if I'm going to be a good agent I will have to overcome my shyness and I feel perfectly safe with you. Where do you want me to sleep tonight?"

"You can have the bed Jasmine I'll sleep on the settee I don't mind and Freddie will protect you he monitors everything, don't you Freddie."

"Yes, James unless you instruct me to turn the cameras off inside the motorhome for privacy."

Jasmine smiled resting her head against James's shoulder. "I'm looking forward to buying new clothes tomorrow James."

James went and showered himself securing a towel around his waist to ensure his modesty was covered. In the meantime Jasmine had removed her towel and slid into the bed and watched James's every movement intently as he went to the front of the motorhome turning his back on Jasmine dressing in fresh clothes.

"I see there's one rule for you and another for me?"

"What you mean Jasmine," James responded coldly.

"Well, you can look at my body and I can't look at yours?"

"I can assure you, you're missing absolutely nothing, I'm just an average guy, now go to sleep Jasmine, that's an order," he smiled.

"Okay bully," she said smiling sliding the blankets off her breasts so James could have full view. He turned away quickly hearing her giggle and he laid down on the settee. So much for sweet and innocent, he thought she was worse than Natasha she was a real tease. The following morning soon arrived. Jasmine had taken it upon herself to make the coffee totally naked. James opened his eyes and shut them quickly before Jasmine realised he'd seen her. She started to rattle the cups trying to make him wake up. She placed the coffee on the table and called out

"James, come on sleepyhead, James I've made the coffee." She waited patiently for him to see her naked James responded without opening his eyes.

"If I open my eyes and you're not fully dressed I'm going to put you over my knee and give you the biggest thrashing you've ever had do you understand me Jasmine?"

"You wouldn't dare, I'd report you."

Mary appeared on the monitor, "yes, he would and he has my approval, get some clothes on now." Jasmine screamed running off to the wardrobe and slipping on her old clothes.

"Sorry James," Mary voiced. "I'll have her replaced she's no bloody good as an agent if she behaves like this."

"Please don't Mary I'm sorry I really want to be a good agent I just got a little carried away teasing James you must admit he's a real handsome guy."

"Your last chance Jasmine providing James is prepared to put up with you after your recent display, what shall we do with her James it's your choice?"

"I don't know? Okay I'll give her one more shot." Mary disappeared from the monitor.

Jasmine kissed James on the lips and then pulled away, "I'm sorry James, I just fancy you like mad and I've only just met you, perhaps it's because you kill people and you're dangerous it excites me, surely you'd like to take me to bed I'm not ugly?"

"I didn't say you were and I didn't say you weren't attractive, I'm married with two children of course you already know that."

"Juliet is bloody lucky to have someone like you." Jasmine exhaled.

They left the motorhome and Freddie drove them to Inverness where Jasmine selected new clothes and shoes for herself; they were gone for most of the day. James spent most of his time surveying the public as they passed wondering how the hell he could possibly know which one of them was a terrorist amongst the thousands of immigrants that had been permitted to enter the country. He thought with a heavy sigh the country would eventually be overrun by foreigners and England would be no more. He lent with his back against the wall waiting for Jasmine to come out of the last shop she'd visited almost all of them he reckoned, and shopping was never one of his strong points for entertainment. They'd been so long that Freddie had to keep moving the car to avoid a parking ticket he said the traffic wardens couldn't work out why every time they walked towards him he moved which made James smile. Jasmine was loaded down with new clothes and a brand-new laptop. James enquired. "Why do you need that? You can use the computer on the motorhome?" I don't like using the firm's computer for Private messages to my friends," she answered. They, returned to the motorhome on entering Juliet appeared on the screen.

"Oh yes James, what have you been up too?" Juliet remarked seeing the young beautiful Jasmine with armfuls of shopping.

"I'll let Mary explain," James exhaled, "whatever I say you will never believe me."

Juliet laughed, "Cheer up my love I already know, I was only teasing." Juliet continued, "How do you like being a field agent Jasmine, working with my husband and I emphasise husband so hands off."

"I know he's your husband you lucky sod, sleeping with him every night must be a dream, if you ever want to get rid of him give me a ring please," Jasmine smiled.

Juliet burst into laughter, "how far did you get with him?" Juliet enquired.

Before Jasmine could drop them both in it James interrupted, "hey you two I'm not a piece of meat and if you're going to talk about me, do it when I'm not around."

Juliet laughed even more, "Oh you're hurting my head and I'm home tomorrow my love. Mary said you'd be leaving there within the next couple of days. If you've been a good boy husband I have something warm waiting for you," James smiled.

Jasmine commented, "He's been a good boy Juliet I can assure you more's the pity." Juliet disappeared from the screen.

James removed his shoes and denim jacket walking over to the bed and laying down. Jasmine rummaged through her new clothes trying on dress after dress flaunting in front of James who didn't take a blind bit of notice she thought. Finally when she thought she had exhausted every avenue of enticement she flopped down on the bed beside him and they both drifted off to sleep. Jasmine woke first and slowly and carefully she unbuttoned James's shirt and gently kissed him on the chest. She moved her hand to the top of his jeans and started to undo his belt he grabbed her hand, "private property love but nice try." James sat up quickly grabbing Jasmine and kissing her on the lips passionately. She thought she had finally won only to be rolled on her back and he slapped her backside several times very hard. She jumped to her feet almost in tears and went to punch James in the face but he caught her wrist in time. "Fucking bastard that was nasty I was only being nice to you."

"I'm not a nice guy Jasmine, get the message I shan't tell you again I'll put a bullet between your eyes."

Jasmine rubbed her backside and went and sat on the settee realising she had pushed James too far and if she wanted to stay in the organisation she would have to play by his rules. James re-buttoned his shirt and made a coffee for them both. He placed both cups on the table and sat beside Jasmine. "What do you expect me to do Jasmine? I know you're attractive, yes I would love to sleep with you, only I'm married and I'm not going to betray Juliet's trust." Jasmine didn't reply and James left the motorhome for a walk along the shoreline. He was gone about an hour in the meantime Jasmine was looking for revenge. She knew how admin worked and had all the passwords to top-secret files. She came across the conversation between Mary and James discussing his sexual encounter with Natasha before she died. This was all the ammunition she needed to achieve her goal she hoped.

James returned to the motorhome to find Jasmine had changed her clothes into a short black see-through nightie. "You don't quit do you Jasmine," James commented.

"Would you care to explain to Juliet why you were fucking Natasha it's all on record?"

"Freddie, turn the internal surveillance off please." James instructed. "Carry on Jasmine I'm listening," James said calmly.

"You slept with Natasha what's wrong with me?"

"Natasha was a mistake a silly mistake which I will have to live with for the rest of my life."

"Well, make a mistake with me I won't say anything."

"You realise Jasmine I could snap your neck in a second or put a bullet in your head and it wouldn't worry me in the slightest so why are you pushing your luck?"

Jasmine exhaled realising she had never been so close to death in her life as she was now, trying to bribe James was not the smartest idea she'd ever had. She watched James storm out of the motorhome and drive off in the Lamborghini. She set up her new laptop quickly plugging in to the main computer on the workstation and downloaded several files, mainly of Juliet and her previous assignments and all the videos she could obtain.

She dressed herself quickly and left the motorhome crossing the road and sitting behind a rock close to the campsite so she would have access to the

Wi-Fi. Jasmine contacted her secret boyfriend Carlo, who was a member of a terrorist organisation. They exchanged a few pleasantries and she told him her plan to piece together a film of Juliet having an affair behind James's back and make out his daughter Fiona was somebody else's so he would be preoccupied with trying to resolve his own issues he wouldn't be paying so much attention to the terrorist operation. Carlo smiled," you are brilliant do whatever you must my love you will be rewarded by our organisation for your contribution."

Jasmine started work immediately piecing together information on Juliet's previous assignments and pictures which had been taken of her naked with previous boyfriends on the bed. She played her conjured film to see what it looked like she thought it was enough to upset James. She also added a voice of Juliet saying James was not the father of their child. She rang James on his mobile he answered, "What do you want I'm still angry with you."

"I just wanted to apologise again James I've been stupid please come and talk to me I have something you ought to see which will prove I am really your friend and why I wanted to sleep with you."

"Okay I'll see you in a minute, he rang off.

Jasmine quickly returned to the motorhome applying her makeup changed her jumper and jeans to a short skirt and see-through blouse without a bra. She poured two large glasses of Scotch as she heard the Lamborghini return she seated herself on the settee cross legged reading a magazine. James entered standing straight in front of her, "well I'm waiting what have you to say your pushing your luck with me Jasmine, "he reaffirmed.

"Tell Freddie to turn off the monitors and not to listen please James," she said quietly.

"Freddie turn off the monitors and don't listen to our conversation," James said firmly.

Freddie replied. "Have done so James," although Freddie had made Mary aware of the situation secretly. Mary told Freddie to record all the conversations and record all events that took place and transmit them to her and her only.

With a shaking hand Jasmine passed James a glass of Scotch he took it from her hand. "You know I've worked in administration James and I want to be a good agent and I thought if I watched some of the video footage privately I would gain experience and make me a better agent for our country."

James listened carefully deciding to sit beside her, "and your point is Jasmine?"

"I thought it was quite normal for agents to sleep together and when on assignments you have to sleep with the enemy am I correct?"

"No, I don't know where you got that idea from Jasmine, "James smiled. "I don't sleep with anybody other than my wife I just shoot people it's easier."

"She sipped her Scotch that's not quite true James you know," she said with a brief smile.

James took a drink from his glass looked at the window and back to Jasmine, "I explained what happened between me and Natasha it was a mistake." he said calmly looking into his glass.

She knew he was feeling vulnerable which was to her advantage and her plans. "Well from all the footage I've watched most of the female agents are in bed with somebody and I'm afraid to say that includes Juliet."

James pulled his gun from his pocket and put it against Jasmine's head, "don't James don't I have the proof."

"What you mean you've got the proof?" He said trying to stop himself pulling the trigger.

Jasmine calmly put her glass on the table and placed her computer on her lap.

"Please don't shoot me James I'm only trying to be honest and helpful I really like you James but if I show you this information you cannot tell anybody otherwise I'll be sacked I'm doing you a favour James and risking my career at the same time. You promise me you won't say anything."

James sighed heavily, "okay you have my word now what's so disturbing you need to show me."

Jasmine took another large sip of whiskey from her glass and switched on her laptop playing James the video of Juliet on a bed talking to someone. James stared in horror then he heard her say not to tell James he was not the father of Fiona. He watched intently seeing shadowy pictures of what appeared to be Juliet making love to a man on a bed and then on another slide Juliet tied to the bed posts laughing, "Turn it off Jasmine I've seen enough." He remarked drinking the remainder of his whiskey in one go.

"Sorry," James she said watching him lower his gun back into his pocket. He sat there with his hands together looking to the table top. Jasmine placed her arm around him and gave him a hug. So you can see why I thought all agents just slept around I was using Juliet's videos for reference and I couldn't understand after you'd been with Natasha why you wouldn't take me to bed."

Jasmine watched the tears forming in James's eyes as he processed the information she had provided. She moved to the kettle and made a coffee for them both while James sat silent. She returned a moment later with 2 cups of coffee. "Remember James you promised me you won't say anything to anyone." She reminded, feeling she had succeeded in deceiving him. He left his coffee removing his jacket and rested on the bed. Jasmine brought his coffee to the bedside table and sat on the edge drinking hers.

Freddie who'd been quietly listening to all the conversations and transmitting the information to Mary who was very disturbed with the whole setup, she wondered what type of game Jasmine was playing and to what ends other than to get James in bed which seem to be her main goal although. Mary wasn't entirely convinced that was the whole plan. Mary studied the footage that Jasmine had shown James. Jasmine had a very high clearance level but shouldn't have had access to all of Juliet's files which she appeared to have. Mary decides to let the situation continue and hoped James was clever enough to work out that he'd been conned.

Juliet appeared on the screen James where are you? James moved from the bed and Jasmine moved to the far end of the settee out of Juliet's vision and released three more buttons on her blouse making sure anyone who saw her would realise she wasn't wearing a bra and could see most of her breasts. "What do you bloody want Juliet I hope I'm not disturbing you."

"What you mean James, Juliet asked shocked seeing the cold expression on James's face."

"I just wondered who was keeping my bed warm while I was away that's all, have you got me any erotic photos you can send me of you and other men?"

"Don't be bloody ridiculous James I'm not a tart thank you, what's brought all this on? Don't you trust me?"

"No, I don't."

Juliet put her hand to her mouth stunned by his reply he watched the tears forming in her eyes she had never known him respond in such a way before. Jasmine eased herself into the view of the monitor. Juliet could easily see her breasts and she switched the monitor off immediately suspecting her husband was having an affair. Jasmine quickly did up the three buttons on her blouse and pulled it together so she was not revealing as much as James turned around.

Juliet contacted Mary and told her what had happened. Mary explained that she already knew and Juliet was to ignore James's comments and she told her the reason why. Juliet was absolutely stunned at Jasmine's attempt to wreck their marriage. but for what reason it must be more than just trying to get James in bed. Mary instructed her, "you are not to let on you know Juliet, what's happening. Whatever takes place you will just have to let things play out. We may have a double agent on our hands and we didn't realise it.

"James, please don't say too much you'll get me dismissed and I'm just starting to enjoy being a field agent."

James briefly smiled and seated himself by Jasmine placing his arm around her shoulder she held his hand, "I wish I hadn't said anything now I feel awfully guilty," she professed trying not to grin.

James kissed her on the head, "no, thank you, it just shows you can't trust anybody Jasmine not even your own wife."

Jasmine released his hand unbuttoning her blouse, "excuse me James I'm being bitten by midges," she moved away from him to the mirror she could see he was watching she quickly removed her blouse looking round her breasts for midges. She knew James could see everything and she was desperately trying not to smile at his attraction to her.

James suggested. "Take a shower Jasmine and see if that improves your discomfort."

"That's a good idea James I think I will."

She removed the remainder of her clothing standing completely naked by the shower so there was nothing he couldn't see and then entered. James heard the water turned on. He quickly grabbed the laptop and opened switching on. Jasmine had been so quick in her preparation to trap James she had failed to put a password in place. He looked at her emails quickly and discovered a message from Carlo asking if she'd been successful in deceiving James and to sleep with him to gain his complete confidence. James realised he'd been had which didn't sit well with him at all and he managed to upset Juliet in the process. Jasmine stepped out of the shower.

"Let me help you Jasmine," James said smiling, he grabbed a dry towel and rubbed her down she was exhilarated by the experience, she felt his hands gliding over her breasts and down her legs. James told her to dress they were going out. She did as he requested immediately.

Freddie drove them in the Lamborghini to the Old Russian anchorage. James held her hand which made Jasmine feel very secure and happy. They entered one of the disused buildings. James turned to face her carefully unbuttoning her blouse which brought a big smile to her face he released her bra. She quickly removed her jeans laying on the hard concrete floor placing her jeans under her head for support. James started making love to her. She was enjoying every moment and insisted he keep going she didn't want him to stop. They dressed, James walked behind her and kissed her on the cheek saying, "sorry," and broke her neck. She didn't feel a thing it was that quick. He checked no one was watching and cast her body out to sea. Freddie didn't ask any questions to the whereabouts of Jasmine as he already knew, he returned James to the motorhome. James contacted Mary and explained what he'd done and why missing out the part she was a double agent. He said she was just a risk to the organisation if she was prepared to bribe him to get her own way and him in bed.

Mary sighed "I'm afraid I have to agree with you James I will list her has falling off a cliff in the line of duty." Although Mary knew James had worked out Jasmine was a double agent but she wasn't prepared to tell him what she knew already.

"As you wish Mary it's your decision."

"Come home James your mission has finished on this occasion I'm sure Juliet will be pleased to see you and of course the children."

James deleted all the information that was on Jasmine's laptop and broke it in half burying it deep in one of the bins on the campsite.

Chapter 23
Homeward Bound

James woke up early the next morning and made some breakfast while Freddie loaded the Lamborghini under the motorhome. James went and said goodbye to the camp warden's Steve and Nicky. James returned to the motorhome and sat back while Freddie took control of the motorhome. James decided he should buy a present for his wife and the children on the way home. He instructed Freddie pull in to Gairloch to see if he could find anything suitable to purchase. It was only a matter of 5 miles away and on route. Freddie parked the motorhome and James started walking through the small village which consisted of half a dozen shops at most. James looked through the window of a very odd shop selling mystical articles very expensive T-shirts and jackets plus a host of ornaments. He entered the shop continually banging his head on the windchimes hanging from the ceiling on very thin cord. The young girl behind the counter had gone to town with the makeup almost imitating a Goth. James concluded it was all part of the illusion trying to get the public in the mood and make them think the articles were all magical. From a dark corner the far side of the shop a woman came into the dim light. James stood paralysed on the spot if it wasn't Natasha it was her ghost. Common sense prevailed he knew she'd been assassinated so there was no chance it was her. He watched her leave the shop and he followed only to find she had disappeared from sight but there was nowhere to hide. James asked Freddie, "you monitoring me Freddie."

"Yes, James."

"Did you see a woman leave the shop she looked exactly like Natasha but we both know she was assassinated?"

"I did see the resemblance James, unlike you I have no emotions it is not possible for the woman to be Natasha."

"Thank you Freddie I thought I was going mad for a moment or perhaps it's my guilty conscience having payback for all my sins."

"Your blood pressure is off the scale James calm yourself and think realistically you know Natasha is dead."

"Perhaps it's her ghost where did she go Freddie?"

"She is behind the shop hiding for what reason I don't know I cannot detect any weapons she may be carrying."

"Do you think she's an agent?"

"I only process programs James I don't possess human intuition although I would say from her behaviour she is troubled."

"I'll investigate Freddie."

"It's no good me telling you not to James, make sure your gun is loaded and be prepared I will notify Mary of the event."

James walked slowly to the back of the shop just as he was to go around the corner the woman went to run he grabbed her arm she struggled he grabbed her other wrist and she kicked him on the shins and then threw him on the floor and stood over him with a large knife.

"Who are you," James asked quickly fearing he was about to be stabbed.

"Why are you following me?" She said with a Russian accent.

James was speechless for a moment trying to work out how this woman could possibly look exactly like Natasha right down to long blonde hair. He went to stand up and she put her stiletto heel on his chest not quite administering enough force to hurt him but was leaving him in no doubt she could kill him.

"Answer my question she said why are you following me?"

"Because you look like someone I knew; Natasha who I was very fond of and died recently."

The woman removed her foot from James's chest and held out her hand assisting him to his feet with a smile, "you are definitely James I wasn't sure to start with."

"Who are you then," James asked very confused.

"My name is Nadia I am Natasha's twin sister."

James lent against the wall in shock. "She never said anything to me about a twin sister and what are you doing here?"

"I'm carrying on from where she left off, we are not convinced you have caught all the terrorists in the area, we suspect there will be another shipment soon and I am here to eliminate them by whatever means."

"There was nothing I could do to save Natasha I'm very sorry for your loss." James said trying to fight back the tears and stop looking like a wimp.

"I have read the file my sister spoke very favourably of you she said you were too nice to be an agent, although like the flick of a switch you would kill someone without a second thought."

James sighed, "would you like a coffee my motorhome is close by I'm sure Mary would love to talk to you."

Nadia nodded and followed James back to the motorhome she sat very proper and official on the settee you could almost sense she would spring into action any second. James commented. "Relax Nadia we are not the enemy."

She smiled nervously searching the motorhome with her eyes and saw the monitor come to life displaying a picture of Mary. Mary started speaking in Russian directly to Nadia; she moved closer to the monitor. Mary and Nadia spoke for nearly half an hour before Mary spoke to James. "How are you feeling James," Mary smiled, "Nadia wasn't aware of your latest elimination, she will travel back with you after she collect's her things I see your blood pressure went off the scale again James."

Nadia laughed, "he thought he seen a ghost."

Freddie spoke, "he is not the only one my circuits are in overdrive trying to work out what is going on."

"I will speak to your boss Nadia and explained everything to him and hopefully we can have a long and fruitful relationship working together."

Nadia smile broadened, "that would be beneficial for both countries we must stop the terrorists otherwise our lives will not be worth living."

Nadia left the motorhome walking across the road to the local hotel she returned half an hour later with her suitcase that looked like it had been through world War three. James made her another coffee and showed her all the facilities were on the motorhome although she commented, "we have the drawings in Russia I know how everything works on here."

James didn't respond he wasn't surprised in the slightest; the only person left in the dark was him he concluded; he was just a killing machine and nothing else. Freddie proceeded heading homeward. James couldn't stop looking at Nadia who had picked up a woman's magazine purchased by

Jasmine. James was convinced there should be some differences in appearance between her and Natasha but he was damned if he could see any. She glanced from the magazine to James, "I'm not that pretty James why are you so fascinated by me?"

"I'm sorry I don't mean to stare at you but I'm trying to see if there is anything different between you and Natasha in appearance, I can't find anything."

Nadia smiled, "I know Natasha was very fond of you James and I know you made love to her shortly before she was assassinated she told me in a text message what a wonderful person you are."

James turned slightly red-faced realising it appeared the whole world knew about him and Natasha. Nadia continued reading the magazine with a grin on her face knowing she had the ability to attract James's attention.

Nadia casually said, not lifting her eyes from the magazine, "You also eliminated one of your own agents, Jasmine. You are truly an assassin without mercy."

James could feel the noose tightening round his neck and suspected Juliet was just waiting for him to come home and put a bullet between his eyes for his indiscretions. Nadia was enjoying every moment of making James feel uncomfortable, almost as if she was trying to punish him. James moved to the back of the motorhome and lay on the bed. Nadia glanced up from the magazine and then continued reading. James just stared at the ceiling he could feel something was not right, he didn't know what. He'd always known his life was like Russian roulette you never know when the bullets in the chamber were heading for you.

Freddie announced. "We are 3 miles away from Dunbar I've booked a one night stopover."

James sat up, "what's the point Freddie we could continue straight home rather than stay out one more night."

"Those are Mary's orders James. You just have time to walk along the beach before nightfall."

Nadia opened her suitcase removing a handgun and a flat pair of shoes, "come on James take me for a stroll," she smiled.

James stood up went to the wardrobe and removed his denim jacket sliding his handgun into one pocket after checking the clip was full. Nadia watched him checking his pockets removing and replacing his handcuffs. She commented, "I hope you're not planning anything kinky James," she smiled placing her handgun in her leather jacket which matched her leather slacks. Freddie asked, "James your blood pressure is high what is the reason, you're not in danger?"

"How would you know Freddie I'm not in danger? You don't know whose going to shoot you in the back."

Freddie didn't respond and sent the information direct to Mary who had been secretly monitoring all the conversations between Nadia and James. She knew if James suspected anything he would shoot first and ask questions later, as he always did regardless of the consequences and spark an international incident by shooting a friendly agent. Mary appeared on the screen with a concerned expression. "James, Nadia is no threat to you do you understand me James?"

Nadia looked immediately at James's expression she could see his cold eyes. She immediately approached him and kissed him on the lips and pulled away looking him straight in his dead eyes. "I don't blame you for my sister's death and I am not here to assassinate you in revenge. We are on the same team James calm down although I know you blame yourself for her death."

"We are trying to establish cooperation from all agencies around the world James and if you shoot someone you shouldn't then all my work will be for nothing" Mary said firmly.

"Perhaps Mary if you bloody told me what was going on and stopped leaving me in the dark all the time I wouldn't get so excited," James shouted.

Mary had never known James to lose the plot he was obviously under pressure and felt threatened. "Okay James I get the message; we must keep as much information as possible from getting into the wrong hands that is why you are told very little in case you are captured and tortured."

James responded quickly, "now that I understand," he smiled continuing, "there'll be an awful lot of dead people before I'm captured Mary."

"Good your blood pressure is coming down James," Mary commented, continuing, "your soon be home and hopefully you'll be able to rest before the next mission materialises. I know you're still extremely upset about Natasha's death and you feel responsible, Mary vanished from the monitor.

They arrived at the campsite and Freddie parked the motorhome so they had full view of the sea. James and Nadia left the motorhome and started walking along the shoreline. Nadia reached for James's hand he glanced down and held her hand feeling the warmth. "You were in love with my sister Natasha weren't you James?" She said releasing his hand and placing her arm around his waist.

"I don't know Nadia in fact I don't know anything any more I've decided. She would get great pleasure out of teasing me and finally I couldn't resist her, if I hadn't have been married to Juliet I would have married Natasha without hesitation."

Nadia kissed James on the cheek he glanced to her with a brief smile of appreciation. "You are not like a normal agent James, there is something special about you which I don't understand myself I can see Natasha's attraction to you I feel the same way although I shouldn't admit it." She said bowing her head staring into the sand for an answer.

James placed his arm around Nadia's waist she lent her head against his shoulder, "I feel comfortable with you James and I've only just met you and you had the same effect on my sister." Nadia paused, turning to face James, holding both his hands searching his brown eyes that once had death written across them. They were about to kiss when James saw a familiar flash of reflection he reached for his gun immediately pushing Nadia to the ground he could see the reflection of the telescopic sights attached to a rifle, he fired four shots; simultaneously, Nadia struggled to her feet quickly and removed her weapon searching the rocks for anyone else. They approached the location of the rifle, finding a man dead from a single shot to the head. Nadia noticed, "James you're bleeding," she pulled his jacket off his shoulder to see a bullet hole in his arm. "That would have killed me James if you hadn't of pushed me to the ground. Come on let's get back to the motorhome and fix you up."

Mary immediately appeared on the monitor very alarmed seeing James had been shot in the arm although the bullet had gone straight through missing all vital arteries. "Oh James I don't understand you, you've just been shot and your blood pressure reads normal you are a strange one." She then focused her attention to Freddie, "what's your excuse Freddie you are supposed to be monitoring these two?"

"I can't see through rock and they were below the embankment so I could only listen until they were visible again."

Nadia pointed her weapon at Freddie's control panel. "You listen to our private conversation which was not work-related?"

"Calm down Nadia, you two are worse than working with children of course Freddie listens to conversations, in case of an emergency but any think that is not relevant to the organisation is dismissed and not held on file."

"I owe James my life Mary he push me out of the line of fire."

"He must like you Nadia otherwise you'd be dead," Mary smiled continuing, "I'll arrange for the body to be collected and see if we can find out who he worked for." Mary paused for a moment, "Nadia don't look into James's brown eyes your mind will go blank," Mary chuckled and the monitor went blank.

"James you are a crazy son of a bitch," Nadia professed then kissed him passionately on the lips and embraced him.

Much to James's surprise Juliet appeared on the monitor just as Nadia moved away. "Mary just told me what's happened James and about Nadia I didn't know Natasha had a twin sister?"

"I didn't know I'm as surprised as you Juliet."

Nadia moved into focus; Juliet put her hand to her mouth, "my God you're identical."

"I'm pleased to see you Juliet, your husband has just saved my life, you should be proud of him."

"I am."

"James how come Jasmine fell off a cliff?"

"She just slipped I think when we were checking out the Russian anchorage again."

James could see Juliet studying his expression to see if he was telling the truth it was obvious she was not convinced by the explanation provided by Mary. "Are you sure James, that's what happened to Jasmine?"

James was becoming annoyed, "no, what really happened is I ripped her clothes off made love to her several times broke her neck and threw her in the sea are you happy now? Sod whether I've been shot or not."

"Okay grumpy I know you're tired and injured Mary told me it wasn't serious only a scratch and keep your hands off Nadia otherwise I'll shoot your balls off when you get home." The monitor went blank.

"She didn't believe your story James about Jasmine falling off a cliff. She would sooner believe you slept with her."

"No, I agree with you Nadia and she would shoot my balls off without thinking twice."

Nadia laughed, "at least you wouldn't have to worry about anyone getting pregnant."

"Let's go out again Nadia I'd like to finish off our stroll along the beach and see if I can find another terrorist, I'm just in the mood to shoot someone it may make me feel better."

"Freddie if I find out you're listening to our private conversations I will blow your circuits out when we return," Nadia said firmly.

James and Nadia left the motorhome again and continued walking along the beach she placed her arm around his waist and he did likewise with his other arm bandaged. James remembered he'd taken the same route with Juliet before she was injured. The moonlight flickered on the advancing waves it was almost dusk. Nadia paused turning to face James she draped her arms around his neck and passionately kissed him again he tried not to respond but couldn't stop himself from placing his one good arm around her pulling her closer to him. "I would like you to make love to me James," Nadia said easing away from him.

"We can't Nadia I'm married and before you remind me, yes I did sleep with your sister and enjoyed every second, now I have to live with the consequences, if Juliet finds out I'm a dead man and she's already suspicious about Jasmine's disappearance."

"You don't fancy me James?"

"That's a stupid bloody question," he smiled.

Nadia smiled, "I'm not going to pressurise you James, you will make love to me when you are ready and you know you're going to."

"Don't Nadia, everyone I get close to dies I'm bad luck and I don't want to see you hurt. Look what happened today I nearly lost you because you weren't paying attention just like Natasha she was more concerned with me than the mission." Nadia didn't reply.

They held hands walking back to the motorhome, Nadia was processing what James had just said and it all made sense. She really wanted to become involved with him but not at the expense of her own life which would make the whole exercise a waste of time. She would have to think of a different approach if she wanted to gain his attention. "I'll sleep on the settee Nadia you can have the bed." Nadia smiled in agreement and after making a coffee she moved to the bed. Removed her clothes entering the shower, James remained on the settee trying not to look at her shapely figure while she removed her garments. James finally fell asleep waking the next morning as Freddie started the motorhome. Nadia was already dressed in a black skirt and white blouse passing James a coffee. They had over 300 miles to travel before James was home and finally in the arms of Juliet if she didn't decide to shoot him.

"Did you sleep okay James?" Nadia enquired trying to make conversation.

"Yes not bad," he said sipping his coffee.

For some unknown reason neither of them wanted to talk really the whole situation seemed awkward not like they'd first met. James continually glanced to Nadia and she did likewise, neither attempted to embrace or even share a kiss. James did notice how properly dressed Nadia was, showing nothing and leaving everything to the imagination which he admired. That was the difference he been looking for between Natasha and Nadia or perhaps Nadia felt she should dress appropriately considering she was about to meet Juliet and didn't want to give her the wrong impression.

Mary appeared on the monitor "Nadia I have arranged for you to stay with James and Juliet now it has been agreed with your director you will work as part of our team for the foreseeable future and you will take orders directly from me Nadia do you understand?"

"Yes Mary providing Juliet or James don't mind me invading their privacy."

"I have already consulted Juliet she is perfectly happy with the arrangements and James will do as he's told, won't you James?"

"I guess so Mary, it looks like you're arranging my life again?"

"I always have James you just haven't realised it. Nadia is going to be your partner, Juliet will stay with the children at home and monitor the situation from the control room."

"I just realised Mary, we don't have enough rooms," James remarked.

"You will have in the next two or three days the builders have already started building an extension. In the meantime, your mother and father have agreed to keep Roger with them until the work is finished."

"Thanks for consulting me Mary,"

"I don't think you realise James, how important the collaboration between agencies is in our fight against terrorism. We are finally making progress and you will not be allowed to interfere." The monitor went blank.

"She wasn't happy," Nadia commented.

"No, you're right, something's happened and she's not letting on."

"It looks like were partners I can't see Juliet agreeing to that proposal easily?"

Not Guilty

"I don't think she would, something as happened and it would have to be serious to make Juliet change her mind."

Nadia dialled a number on her mobile and started speaking in Russian, James watched the expression change on her face and tears form in her eye which she tried to hold back. Nadia glanced to James and lowered her mobile to her lap very slowly.

"What's happened Nadia?"

"My mother and father have been executed by a terrorist."

James immediately embraced her trying to give her comfort, James vowed, "I will find them Nadia and kill them."

She pulled away from James holding both his hands sniffling, "that's not all James. Brace yourself, your son Roger and your mother and father have also been executed. She burst into tears. They held each other in a flood of tears and heartbreak. James phoned Juliet and she didn't answer, he asked Freddie to contact her. "I am not permitted James those are Mary's instructions. There is a total blackout on communications from now on until further notice."

"Do you know if Juliet is safe and Fiona?" Freddie didn't reply for half an hour.

Freddie, without any explanation suddenly started driving faster. James went to the front of the motorhome looked at the speedometer the motorhome was now travelling just over 90 miles an hour Freddie advised "Mary will speak to you in a minute James we have to return you home quickly you are needed and so am I."

James feared the worst he was sure whatever Mary had to say would not be good news. Nadia was still drying her eyes and James returned to join her she tried to contact her boss again only to discover he wasn't answering which was something he never failed to do.

"James what's going on," she sobbed.

James embraced Nadia and kissed her on the forehead although his own heart had been torn away he was determined there would be payback in a way the terrorists had never seen he wanted revenge big-time. "I don't know Nadia we'll know more when Mary talks to us but I want some bloody answers," he said drying his eyes. James's mobile rang he stood up and answered.

"James I don't know what to say." He could tell Mary was sobbing and that's something he never known her do in all the time he'd known her.

"Mary, give it to me straight."

"Put your phone on speaker so Nadia can hear." James did immediately sitting down by her.

"Your suspicions regarding Jasmine were spot on. We were going through her files and one of the technicians unknowingly activated a Trojan horse she had planted in case she died. The Trojan horse automatically sent your location, Nadia's parents and several other operatives all the information went direct to a terrorist organisation before we realised what had happened. Once we realised how serious the situation was we shut down our operation and notified every other organisation around the world and most did the same as we did shut down until we could establish the extent of the damage and who was in danger."

James and Nadia looked at each other and sighed heavily. James asked, "How many of my family are alive Mary? and why is Freddie driving like his circuits are on fire?"

"Freddie is the only independent workstation we have. Freddie realised what Jasmine was doing from the motorhome's workstation, once she had finished receiving the information she wanted. Freddie broke the link realising he could be contaminated and he conveyed his concerns to me, in the meantime you had disposed of Jasmine which was a shame in some respects, we may have been able to extract valuable information from her."

"Where's, Juliet and Fiona?"

"Juliet and Fiona are in lockdown in the bungalow, she realised one of the workmen was carrying a gun so she took Fiona and herself into the workstation and activated lockdown. Unfortunately Jasmine had transmitted the override code to the bungalow's front door and there are three terrorists inside. Once Juliet realised the codes were compromised she change the codes and the front door was locked and they can't get out. We have surrounded the bungalow and await Freddie's return so he can scan and see if he can see what's going on inside."

"At least Juliet's still alive and Fiona, thank God for small mercies. I personally will deal with these terrorists their on my turf and that's somewhere you don't want to be when I'm pissed off. I'll give you a free demonstration Mary of me angry."

"Include me in the operation," Nadia voiced, "I have a score to settle too," she sobbed.

Not Guilty

"The police have been instructed to clear the area using the excuse of a major gas leak. They are clearing the junctions on your route so Freddie is not hindered in his progress, Freddie how long before you arrive?"

"10 minutes," Freddie replied.

James went to the back of the motorhome trying to stay on his feet as Freddie drove the motorhome at high speed. Nadia followed James to the weapons cabinet which automatically opened and James instructed Nadia to wear a protective vest if she was coming on the operation with him. She didn't argue they both kitted themselves out ready for war and it was going to be one hell of a war.

Finally they arrived outside the bungalow. Mary came aboard kissed James and Nadia on the cheek. Mary's make-up had run down the side of her cheeks from where she'd been crying over the loss of her godchild. "Scan the bungalow Freddie."

Freddie did so immediately displaying the infrared images of three people wandering around the living room and occasionally trying to smash the door on the control room in the corridor. James and Nadia both checked their weapons and left the motorhome without saying another word. The police stepped aside James instructed Nadia to stay by the front door in case any of the terrorists got past him. He quietly opened the front door, threw in four flash-grenades and charged in as if the devil himself was riding on his back. James shot two of the terrorists in the head the third one had been stunned by a grenade on the floor. James grabbed him by the hair kicking the gun from his hand and dragged him out of the front door. James removed his knife. Shouted to Freddie, "video and transmit to a terrorist website so they can see what happens if they piss me off. James drew his knife down the face of the screaming terrorist then from his throat down to his waist peeling his clothes off as if he was skinning an animal.

Mary shouted at him "stop James you're going too far." James didn't listen he stabbed his knife in behind the terrorist's knee cutting the sinews which sent his leg dead and useless James threw the terrorist to the floor, wiping his knife on his trousers. Nadia watched in horror and holstered her gun. James ran back inside banged on the control room door. "Juliet love, it's me James."

Juliet looked through the spy hole with relief hearing James's voice. She opened the door and flung her arms around him bursting into tears.

"I've never been so scared in my life James, I thought Fiona and I were going to die."

"Not while I'm still breathing love," he said calmly as if this was an everyday occurrence.

Nadia entered the room and went straight over and picked up Fiona taking her out into the fresh air James walked out of his trashed bungalow carrying distraught Juliet into the motorhome where Nadia was playing with Fiona. Freddie in his wisdom had started playing nursery rhymes for Fiona who appeared to be totally oblivious to what had taken place and was quite happy to sit on Nadia's knee, "giggling."

Freddie spoke, "James I'm not permitted to transmit the video without Mary's express permission."

Nadia handed Fiona over to Mary who burst into tears holding her goddaughter very close.

Juliet moved close to Nadia and embraced her, "I knew your sister only for a short while but she was a wonderful person and I was very fond of her."

"Thank you Juliet we have all lost today."

James commented, "you are human after all Mary," he smiled, and as the adrenaline left his body he assessed his losses, mother, father and son. He burst into tears like everyone else.

Chapter 24
Trying to start over

Nadia flew back to Russia to attend her parent's funeral. James and Juliet resided in a hotel in Stratford while repairs were made to the bungalow. James's parents and Roger were all cremated at a very private ceremony attended by Mary and a few others. After the funeral Mary took James aside and spoke privately to him. "James I know what happened between you and Jasmine you didn't tell me the whole truth."

James frowned, "the pictures you saw of Juliet were fabricated by Jasmine surely you couldn't imagine Juliet taking part in filming such an event?"

"I don't know what the truth is any more Mary tell me the truth."

Mary was surprised at his response, "James you know I can't tell you everything that goes on, it would be a breach of security but I can assure you Juliet had nothing to do with the photos."

"I realise she wasn't an angel before I married her Mary, but some of the photos were shocking."

"And what about yourself James you're no blue-eyed boy."

"That's a fact," he said glancing across and looking to Juliet watching the two of them.

"James, you're a fool if you let Juliet go; she loves you so much and she can't understand why you are acting strange."

"If you never trust me again James believe me I am telling you the truth now."

"Okay, if you say so."

"Anyway, Nadia is returning this evening she will be landing at Birmingham airport I want you to meet her there with Freddie. I can't tell you anything about the mission yet I will enlighten you when I have the full details, she is landing at 7:30.

James walked across to Juliet who was holding Fiona. "It looks like I'm on a mission, I've got to collect Nadia from the airport. Don't ask me what the mission is because Mary won't tell me, perhaps she'll tell you."

Juliet tried to smile with her red eyes from crying. "I love you James and I don't know what I've done to upset you. I've never been unfaithful to you James please believe me."

"We're all upset Juliet we've lost a great deal lately," he said kissing her and Fiona on the cheek. "Just let things settle; it will be fine once you're back in the bungalow, you'll feel better."

Freddie appeared from around the corner with the motorhome. Juliet stared towards the vehicle as if she wanted to blow it off the face of the earth. She watched James climb aboard, he turned and gave a slight wave to her; she smiled briefly wondering if it would be the last time she ever saw her husband alive. Mary walked over to join her placing her arm around Juliet's shoulder, "don't worry Juliet it will all work out I just wish James would stop thinking about those bloody photos."

"He's going to leave me Mary I'm sure. I know he loves me in his own way I just hope Nadia doesn't take him to bed I don't think I could stand it."

Mary guided Juliet and Fiona to her car, "come on I'll take you back to the hotel just a few more days and you'll be home."

Suddenly James ran from the motorhome leaning his head through the window he kissed Juliet on the lips "I love you, see you soon," and ran off back to the motorhome. Juliet laughed and cried at the same time.

"See I told you Juliet," Mary laughed driving off. Freddie drove to Birmingham airport and they waited for Nadia to clear customs. She was being held up and asked a hundred and one questions by an officer. James intervened flashing his security card the officer backed off. He held Nadia's hand and led her out of the airport carrying her bag, she smiled "thank you James."

"Your welcome, how are you feeling Nadia?"

"I'm okay James, I didn't see much of my parents I was always on a mission somewhere and Russian children are taught from an early age to stand on their own two feet," she smiled entering the motorhome.

"Hello Nadia," Freddie said.

"I will still blow your circuits out if you listen to our conversations," she smiled.

"What's the assignment James, do you know?"

"No, Mary hasn't told me which is rather odd."

Mary spoke over the intercom, "you're going to Long Marston airfield where you will park up in the hanger. We suspect between six and eight terrorists will be collected. They are coming in on a light aircraft, do not permit the aircraft to take off again James, Nadia, do you understand me.

"Yes Mary," Nadia replied. Freddie drove to Long Marston airfield which was used in world war two. Freddie reversed the motorhome inside a large hanger, James and Nadia closed the doors which made the building very dark inside. They boarded the motorhome; Nadia made them both a coffee and they sat on the settee together. "There is something bothering you James," Nadia enquired.

"Yes, something I saw," he didn't elaborate.

Nadia sipped her coffee, "you mean the digitally enhanced photos and film showing Juliet naked?" She queried.

"How the bloody hell do you know?" James looked horrified realising someone else knew other than Mary himself and Juliet.

"Freddie," Nadia instructed, "turn the heating up, I'm cold in here and turn off internal surveillance altogether or I will shoot you and I'm not joking."

As you requested," Freddie replied.

"In answer to your question James the pictures were sent via the Trojan horse to our headquarters set up by Jasmine."

"Shit, I didn't realise, she was a right bitch although to look at her you couldn't wait to get her in bed."

"Carlo was her contact he has since been shot by me," she smiled, continuing, "if you really want to see what a bitch she was I'll show you."

"Go on cheer me up," James sighed.

"Freddie," Nadia said then spoke to him in Russian.

"He can't understand Russian can he?"

"Yes, now watch the monitor."

"That's Jasmine who is she screwing?"

"That is my boss in Russia but he wasn't there at all he was in his office. Jasmine had enhanced, chopped and edited, using your own technology against us. She created this short scene. She was actually being screwed by Carlo. They tried to bribe my boss, which didn't work so they sent the digital film to his wife." Nadia said something else in Russian to Freddie. "Watch the screen there's my boss and you see the cut across his forehead that is where his wife hit him with a spade.

James burst out laughing, "oh my God."

"Now do you feel better James," Nadia asked, Freddie to turn the monitor off.

"I do, thank you and thank your boss for sharing such a sensitive piece of information."

"He has never met you James but he likes the way you work and it was his idea to show you, otherwise I'd be shot I wouldn't have had access to the information."

"So Juliet wasn't in any of the pictures I saw?"

"That is classified," she laughed.

"You devil," he said placing his hands either side of Nadia's face and kissing her passionately on the lips which she didn't expect.

"I'm your partner and it is my job to look after you, as it is yours to look after me. So whatever happens we have each other's back, we must trust each other without question for the relationship to work."

James nodded in agreement kissing her passionately again on the lips and she responded with absolute approval of his action.

Nadia stood up and removed her coat now she was warm." I'm going to take a shower, there is nothing on satellite for us to worry about Freddie is there?"

"No, Nadia there is nothing within 200 miles to concern us at the moment."

"Good I will shower and change."

James watched Nadia remove her clothing every inch reminded him of Natasha, she glanced back to see the smile on his face as he studied her body. "You can join me if you wish James? You are my partner and what happens between us is private and always will remain so," she confirmed. James was very tempted although he just buried his son and parents it didn't seem right plus he would be cheating on his wife who he'd been punishing for photos that had nothing to do with her.

Nadia smiled and entered the shower alone knowing it wouldn't be long before he would take his pleasure with her. Nadia finished showering and returned to James wearing her dressing gown, seated herself on his lap placing her arm around his shoulder. "What are you doing Nadia? What happens if Mary appears on the screen or Juliet for that matter?"

"Easy fix," Nadia said standing up and walking over to the shower picking up a towel and throwing it over the screen of the monitor returning to James's lap kissing him on the lips.

"Are all Russian girls as forward as you?"

"In Russia we are taught if you want something go and get it before somebody else does, and what are we going to have to eat Freddie?" Nadia asked.

It is not my responsibility to feed you, you should bring your own provisions I am just the transport," Freddie replied.

"Freddie I'll take the Lamborghini and go to the shop before it closes," James suggested, feeling if he stopped here any longer Nadia would have his trousers off.

"Yes, James I'll remove the car." James drove to the local village finding the chip shop open he bought a selection of groceries and fish & chips and returned as quickly as he could to Nadia, who was holding the fort while he was away. They sat at the table eating fish & chips which she enjoyed immensely. "They are not as good in our country as they are in yours," she commented, drinking a glass of Scotch which she poured earlier, in fact half the bottle was empty by the time James returned. James asked "Freddie is there anything on the radar yet?"

"No, James you might as well rest I will wake you both in plenty of time if I detect anything."

James didn't know whether he was excited or scared to death to get into bed with Nadia he had mixed feelings of guilt and excitement. Nadia removed her dressing gown drinking the remainder of the Scotch in her glass and slid into bed looking at James who didn't know whether to sleep on the settee or join his new partner. "Come James, Freddie will say nothing or record anything."

James slid into bed and Nadia immediately started kissing him passionately until she had finally aroused him and she moved herself on top of him starting to making love to him. She just wouldn't leave him alone she continually aroused him until he had made love to her three times. James thought he would sooner have taken on 10 terrorists than be ravished by Nadia, he was absolutely knackered. She was passionate and insistent she knew what she wanted and took it. "Now you feel better James and more relaxed," she said kissing him again on the lips. Nadia kissed him once more and cuddled close to him and they both drifted off to sleep.

Freddie switched all the lights on in the motorhome, "dress quickly, I have detected explosives and someone is approaching the perimeter of the airfield."

"Where are the explosives," Nadia asked quickly.

"They appear to be underneath the motorhome."

"We'd better leave quickly Nadia," James said heading for the door.

"No, Freddie responded it's too late stand on the red spot, both of you now."

James and Nadia did exactly as Freddie had instructed suddenly they were surrounded in foam as the motorhome filled itself. There was an almighty explosion. James woke up in hospital seeing Juliet sitting by his bedside holding Fiona. "Where's Nadia," James asked concerned.

Juliet smiled and kissed him on the forehead, "she's in the other room still unconscious the last I heard."

"The last thing I remember is being encased in foam."

"Freddie saved your lives the motorhome is a total write-off. The explosion blew the vehicle in half how you two ever survived no one will ever know."

Mary came rushing in, "he's awake good," she said brightly continuing, "I have a bill here for you, for just over 2 ½ million pounds for wrecking my motorhome, Lamborghini and killing Freddie, you'll be working for me for the rest of your life before you pay the bill James Thompson," she smiled.

The door opened and another bed was pushed in containing Nadia, "I thought you two would be bored looking at four walls so I've arranged for you both to stay in the same room," Mary smiled.

"What went wrong Mary," James asked on a more serious note.

"It was a trap planned some time ago to lure us into believing terrorists were coming into the country. They buried a large quantity of explosives under the floor of the hangar and placed a stealth coating over the top which Freddie struggled to scan through for a while."

"How long have we been, unconscious Mary."

"About two weeks and you're not entitled to sick pay so get off your arse quickly and start earning your salary."

James glanced to Nadia, "I'm coming to work in your country Nadia my boss is turning into a tyrant."

Not Guilty

Nadia smiled, "you do make my life exciting James; before I met you everything was so simple."

"The bungalow is finished James and Nadia's room is ready; you should be coming home hopefully in the next couple of days; the pair of you of course Juliet said smiling."

James indicated to Mary come closer which she did expecting him to whisper something in her ear instead he placed his hand behind her head and planted a big sloppy kiss on her lips. She pulled away red-faced. How dare you if you weren't ill I'd hit you." She said trying not to smile.

"Sorry Mary I just want to whisper something in your ear it's personal."

Mary bent forward again James whispered in her ear "I love you," then grabbed her head again and kissed her on the lips. She stormed off out of the room.

Three days later Nadia and James were transported to James's bungalow to convalesce for a further two weeks. Nadia's room had been kitted out with her own personal computer and phone so she could talk to anyone in Russia privately when she felt the need. Nadia spent a great deal of time playing with Fiona who seemed to have taken a shine to her. Juliet asked, "you're not getting broody are you Nadia?"

Nadia smiled, "I would love to have a child but we are not permitted and if I became pregnant they would make me have an abortion."

Juliet placed her arm around Nadia, "we had a similar policy in our organisation but thanks to Mary the rules got bent, James and I were allowed to marry. You can always hold and cuddle Fiona, James and I won't mind."

"You are kind Juliet, we are like a family."

"Mary hasn't called in for a long time. James must've really upset her when he kissed her, she's funny like that," Juliet said making a drink for them both.

Mary walked in through the door. "Speak of the devil," Juliet said grabbing another cup for Mary.

"Where is James," Mary asked.

"He's in the control room, why," Nadia asked.

"None of your bloody business," Mary said walking straight past them both to the control room calling back, "do not disturb me." Mary slammed the door behind her which made James jump. Juliet and Nadia went to the control room door trying to listen to what was being said to James. "You are a bloody hypocrite James what the hell do you think you're doing.

When Nadia was in hospital the doctors informed me she had recently had intercourse and the only person that can be is you."

"Hang on Mary, it's wasn't my fault entirely."

"It takes two to tango James, whichever way you look at it, if she's pregnant God help you sunshine because he's the only person that will. I will personally give Juliet a gun to shoot you." Mary pulled the control room door open quickly catching Nadia and Juliet standing outside with red faces. "Nadia in here now, Juliet go away."

Nadia came in the control room Mary slammed the door shut, "are you on the pill?"

"Yes why," Nadia said folding her arms and glaring at Mary.

"So since your accident and being unconscious you haven't taken your pill?"

"I started as soon as I was conscious, what's the bloody problem Mary." Nadia asked.

"How will I explain to your director one of my agents made you pregnant that will really put a spanner in the works."

Juliet came into the room, "what's going on Mary? If it involves James it involves me."

"Did I invite you to this conversation Juliet and you've been more trouble than you're worth all the time' you jealous little bitch."

Juliet left the room in tears. James remarked, "be careful Mary, your pushing our friendship just a little too far."

Mary glared at James, "how, would you like to spend the rest to your life in prison for multiple murders James, don't threaten me."

"I'm going back to Russia I don't need this crap, I'm sure my director would give you employment, leave the old woman to solve her own problems."

"You will stay here Nadia and do as I tell you."

"You will not treat me like dirt I am an agent of the USSR and if you really want an international incident I will give you one. You have nothing on me like we have on you. Yes we know what happened to your husband," Mary staggered backwards in shock. "Your husband had no morals we have photographs, would you like to see them Mary? I'm sure the press in England would be very interested." Mary left the room with her head bowed she had finally met her match in Nadia. Juliet came running in whatever's happened? Mary's gone outside crying, jumped in her car and driven off.

"Come on James what's going on?"

Nadia looked to James. "She was blaming us for the motorhome being blown up saying we weren't paying attention. James warned her for upsetting you and she threatened to have him thrown in prison for murder, I told her a few home truths about her husband."

"Blimey, let's go and have a coffee, better still let's have a glass of whiskey I think we all need one."

Nadia smiled, "that is the best idea I've heard today."

"I suppose I'd better wait for the police to turn up," James commented.

"Don't worry James, she will do nothing, her reputation would be ruined if she did," Nadia commented continuing, "you are my partner and I will protect you from her."

They returned to the front room and each had a large glass of Scotch, sitting on the settee watching Fiona in her playpen. Mary returned an hour later walking into the bungalow. "James, Nadia in the control room please. Juliet, stay here with Fiona. James and Nadia followed Mary into the control room and she shut the door. "I'm sorry I shouldn't have shouted at either of you. I just hope you're not pregnant Nadia. I'm under a lot of pressure from the top to make this work, please help me, otherwise the terrorists are going to win hands down if we argue amongst ourselves."

"Yes, no problem," James commented.

Nadia placed her arm around James's shoulder, "count me in. James and I work well together," she said kissing him on the cheek.

Mary joked. "Less of that and more bang, bang, please Nadia."

James and Nadia laughed. Mary opened the door, "Juliet coming here please." Juliet entered the room nervously. Mary kissed her on the cheek "I'm sorry I was horrible to you," she said smiling.

James commented "I haven't shot a terrorist at least for a month Mary, I'm getting bored."

"I'll have a coffee Juliet, if you kindly make me one," said Mary.

They return to the living room and Mary picked up Fiona from the playpen sitting her on her knee, wishing she had handled the situation better than she did. She knew she had three of the best agents in the world under her control and if she wanted the best from them she would have to treat them with respect. "The Treasury has approved a replacement motorhome and Lamborghini which is good news for us otherwise we'd be without a mobile unit," she commented kissing Fiona on the forehead.

"I hope they fit Freddie back into the system Mary," James stated.

"Most definitely James, he saved you and Nadia from certain death at the cost of his own destruction," she smiled realising she was treating the computer as a person and not software.

Mary's mobile rang; she answered, walking to the far side of the room after passing Fiona to Nadia. They watched the expression on her face change as she received the information the phone call ended. She looked to Nadia saying calmly, "come with me to the control room." Nadia was concerned and followed Mary she shut the door quietly behind them, "sit down Nadia please. There's no easy way to tell you my friend. Your remaining brother has been killed in a road accident, although your director is investigating to see if there are any suspicious circumstances."

Nadia was close to her brother; she sat there in silence. Mary placed an arm around Nadia's shoulder "I'm sorry, as if you hadn't had enough grief you must fly home of course and make arrangements. James will take you to the airport so pack a bag and hopefully we will see you soon."

Nadia kissed Mary on the cheek saying nothing, Mary returned to the living room and told James and Juliet. Nadia said goodbye to Juliet, kissing Fiona on the cheek and James drove Nadia to the airport. James embraced Nadia, "I have no one left James my family are gone all of them."

"You will always have me Nadia, you are my partner and I shouldn't say this, someone I really love."

Nadia smiled, "thank you." holding back the tears of grief.

James watched her disappear into the airport and steadily drove back home. When he arrived Mary had already gone. Juliet embraced him, "how much grief are we expected to withstand James everybody's dying around us, our own family our friends, when will it ever end?"

Chapter 25

Missing Agent

A month had drifted by and Nadia had not contacted either James or Juliet. Mary was becoming concerned; she'd been in touch with Nadia's director. He said he didn't know where she was although Mary wasn't convinced he was telling the truth. Mary came to see James and Juliet and of course her goddaughter which was her main reason for travelling the distance. They sat at the breakfast bar drinking coffee. Mary commented, "Very odd Nadia hasn't contacted me, I'm not convinced her director is telling me the truth."

Juliet remarked, "Isn't she chipped like us so surely we can track her?"

"Apparently her chip is not working or has been removed or damaged." Mary said drinking her coffee.

"I'll fly to Russia I'll find her."

"You will not James. You will not interfere in Russian politics that would really put a cat among the pigeons."

"Well, we just can't do nothing Mary she's one of our team regardless if she's Russian or not, "James remarked rubbing his forehead.

"There must be a way to find her we'll just have to think of it, I'll hack into the Russian surveillance cameras around where her brother lived," Juliet said concerned.

"You really want to start a war Juliet?" Mary commented continuing, "they would know in an instant what was going on."

"Okay, I'll check the airport security cameras here and see if she has returned," Juliet said firmly walking off to the control room.

Juliet surveyed hours of footage on all the airports in the UK, she spent nearly a week in the control room and finally a camera revealed

Nadia landing two weeks ago at Birmingham airport. Juliet immediately told James and Mary. They now feared she'd been captured by terrorists or eliminated. Mary sat and thought for a moment, "if she was dead, the terrorist organisation would want to publicise they had killed another agent, so she's still alive somewhere."

James studied the footage Juliet had found, he remarked, "there's something odd about the picture and I just can't put my finger on it," James said frustrated. Juliet studied the surveillance cameras around Birmingham trying to see if she could find where Nadia had gone, "look, look James she's getting on a bus for Stratford-upon-Avon, she is here right under our noses." Juliet said excited.

"We can't be sure Juliet," James remarked. "There are many stops between here and Stratford. Why hasn't she contacted us, what is she afraid of? I can't believe Nadia is frightened of anything."

"No, I agree with you James," Juliet frowned.

"Let's leave Mary out of the picture for now Juliet, I want to find her, perhaps she is on the run from somebody or her own agency and if we can help we must."

"I'll have to stay in the control room James. You will have to search alone; otherwise Mary will wonder what's going on if no one's on duty."

"Okay love I'll see what I can find out." James took the car and drove to Stratford, parking in the multi-storey car park. He started walking around the shopping centre without having any success. He then ventured to the old town where there were rooms to let and continued into the park seeing a woman resembling Nadia throwing bread to the ducks. He approached cautiously not wishing to cause alarm to anyone. He stood a few yards away and glanced to the woman who he was convinced was Nadia. She didn't look towards him, "you've found me James as I suspected you would eventually. I suppose you'd like an explanation?"

"What's wrong Nadia? Why haven't you come to see us? We're your friends whatever the problem."

"I'm hiding from everyone, I am no longer an agent I have my own life to lead and I just want to be left alone."

"If that's the case, what the bloody hell are you doing living on my doorstep?"

"Because I thought that would be the last place you'd search and that includes my own director."

Not Guilty

James noticed Juliet approaching across the grass carrying Fiona. "I couldn't stay at home, it was doing my head in. Nadia what's wrong you're my friend I don't want to lose you."

James saw a man in a smart suit approaching, heading straight for Nadia. James drew his gun the man stopped in his tracks, "she is to come with me the director's sent me to fetch her."

"Over my dead body, now fuck off before I blow your brains out," James instructed continuing, "take Nadia with you Juliet I'll deal with him."

The Russian agent put his hands up and approached James "I am not here to hurt her, just return Nadia back to her country."

Juliet called back to James. "Nadia is pregnant and their trying to make her have an abortion. Shoot the bastard."

"Government policy James you have the same rules here," the Russian agent said firmly.

Mary appeared, as if things couldn't get any worse James thought, making a beeline for the Russian agent. She spoke to him in Russian. Nadia interpreted for Juliet to understand. Mary is telling him that the child is British and the rules have changed here since you were permitted to have a child. Apparently my director had cancelled the extraction order for me to be taken back to Russia. The agent wasn't aware of the change of orders. The agent shook Mary's hand and walked away. Mary walked over to Nadia and Juliet. James put his gun away and joined them. Juliet said to Mary, "Mary, hold Fiona for me, just for a second." Juliet turned to face James kicked him in the balls and broke his nose with her fist. "You cheating good for nothing bastard," she shouted.

James was on the ground in excruciating pain holding his testicles with one hand and his broken bleeding nose with the other. Nadia spoke, "it wasn't his fault, strike me. I chased him until he gave in. He didn't make love to me L made love to him. I am not ashamed of what I've done he has given me a beautiful child to love now I have no more family left alive.

Mary commented "That serves you right James you've had that coming for a long time."

"I'll help you Nadia," Juliet said taking Fiona from Mary walking back to James's van, which she used to come into town.

"What about James? You won't leave him surely Juliet."

"We'll see, you come home with me, have you seen a doctor to check if everything alright?"

No, I haven't had chance I've been too busy running away from everybody. You would have never known if I'd had my way. I would have kept it a secret to protect you both from heartbreak."

"How far along are you?" Juliet asked concerned.

"I can tell you exactly when I conceived, when the motorhome exploded. I'd spent most of the evening showing James how the pictures taken of you were false and now look what happens I've only made matters worse."

James returned to the car park feeling sick with pain although he knew he'd brought it on himself. He made his way to the local hospital where they fixed his nose. He decided he wasn't going home to face Juliet and she probably wouldn't let him in anyway, to be quite honest he didn't blame her at all. James purchased some clean clothes and booked himself into a local hotel. Mary phoned. "Have you recovered James?"

"I'm okay Mary," he said feeling sick and coughing up blood.

"Good, drive to Dover and look out for a lorry marked, 'International Express', it's due to land in six hours, follow. We suspect firearms are stored on-board we want to know where they're going."

"Okay Mary no problem, are they linked to terrorists?"

"We don't know James that's the whole point."

Mary contacted Juliet instructing her to monitor James's progress, although she would probably want to shoot him herself. Juliet responded, "I think I may have been a little hard on James Mary. If I'd been shown pictures of him naked with other women I probably would have done something stupid to get my own back."

"That's a sensible conclusion Juliet, that doesn't excuse his actions, although I do know he's been distressed over the photos. How is Nadia settling in?"

"She's okay, the firm's doctor came and looked at her, she's progressing nicely and possibly has twins. She has spoken to her director who actually congratulated her on her pregnancy, which I thought was strange. All seems to be hunky-dory again."

"Good," Mary rang off.

James drove to Dover and sat waiting for the lorry patiently, wondering whether he dare ring Juliet and try to smooth things over. He saw the lorry leave the ferry and within half an hour leaving the docks. He placed his binoculars on the passenger seat and checked his clip was full of bullets. James followed the lorry at a discreet distance along the motorway. At the next junction the lorry left the motorway. James stayed as far back as he dare trying not to give away his surveillance position. Seeing the lorry turn off down a farm track, James parked the car and cut across the fields hiding behind the cattle shed. He could hear the men talking which appeared to be in Arabic. That was the last thing James remembered until he woke up locked in the container, he'd found himself bound and gagged. Mary contacted Juliet informing her, chips in every agent had been compromised. Somehow the terrorists had managed to work out the frequency and were tracking us. Juliet was alarmed, "what about James? He doesn't know."

"I think he does Juliet, we fear he may have been captured; his mobile has been destroyed," Mary advised.

"We have sent a signal to all agency chips so they will malfunction and become inoperative until we have a way of stopping this happening again."

Nadia, who was listening to the conversation said," I will find my partner. I should have been with him this wouldn't have happened."

"For once Nadia, stay where you are you're in no condition to take on terrorists. If you lost the baby, you nor James would ever forgive yourselves."

"Neither would I," Juliet said quickly.

"He is my partner, my friend I must go Mary."

"Juliet if she tries to leave shoot her in the bloody leg, I'm not arguing with her anymore."

"In Russia we would not care about being pregnant we would do our duty."

"Tough, you chose to get pregnant in England, you will obey our rules," Juliet enforced.

Nadia went over and sat on the floor playing with Fiona.

James had managed to stand on his feet and hop to the doors looking out through a crack into the darkness. He could see one man leaning against a girder smoking a cigarette. James started feeling his way around the container in the dark trying to find anything he could use to free his hands. Stumbling across a jagged edge where the container had been bashed by a forklift at some time in its life. Luckily they had used ties to bind his wrists which didn't take long to cut through, he then released his feet and finally removed the tape from his mouth. James squeezed his fingers through the container doorway and slowly lifted the catch. He scanned the area in the dark from the container not wishing to step out into a blaze of gunfire. The terrorist who'd lent against the girder was now taking a pee against the hedge. James as quietly as he could, opened the door and squeezed out, carefully shutting and locking it. He knew he was in no position to take the terrorists on in his present condition. He quickly made his way across the fields back to the main road. The terrorists had taken his car to the farm. He thumbed a lift quickly finally being picked up by a van driver who dropped him off in a nearby village, after James explained he just come out of hospital after an accident. James phoned Mary and gave the layout of the farm. She immediately arranged for him to be collected and sent an armed team in to deal with the terrorists. James was taken back to headquarters where he hadn't been for a long time. Mary greeted him as he arrived steering him into her office and poured him a large Scotch. "She really did thump you James. I think she's a better agent than you are, punishing you with that amount of force"

"Like you said Mary, I had it coming for a long time," he said wiping the blood from his mouth where they'd beaten him.

"You hurt anywhere else James," Mary enquired.

"Only where Juliet kicked me, I'm black and blue."

Mark, another agent entered the room. "Take James to hospital I want him checked out"

James was driven to the hospital and examined immediately by a doctor who discovered James had three cracked ribs and was admitted with suspected internal bleeding, Mary phoned Juliet. "James is in theatre he has internal bleeding two or three cracked ribs, but you did more damage to him than the terrorists the doctor told me. It was a miracle he could actually move he must have been in excruciating agony all the way through the assignment and still he didn't complain. James is a hero Juliet," Mary concluded.

"We'll come and see him straightaway."

"Don't Juliet, please. I don't think he wants to see you at the moment he's so ashamed of letting you down,"

Mary could hear Juliet sobbing "it's no good crying over spilt milk Juliet, what's done is done, just give him time."

Mary went to see James in the recovery room she seated herself beside the bed holding his hand. "Mary," he joked. "We'll get talked about."

"Shut up James, the doctors told me you must rest for at least a month otherwise the repairs they carried out inside will tear and could kill you."

"That would be the best thing that could happen. I only bring death and destruction to all the people I love, I'm only good for one thing, killing people."

"I'll come and see you again James when you stop feeling sorry for yourself, you big wuss."

"James indicated with his hand come closer. "You're not catching me out again James, sorry," Mary smiled. "You will be here for a week I'll notify Juliet?"

"No, from now on I'm working on my own and living on my own, that way no one will get hurt that shouldn't."

Mary left. James asked for a piece of paper from one of the nurses and a clipboard. He sat and wrote his will out leaving everything to Juliet and £50,000 to Nadia explaining how much he loved them both and he was sorry for all the upset he caused them both. James sealed the letter in an envelope and addressed it to Juliet, placing it on the bedside locker. James drifted off to sleep. Mary in the meantime had advised Juliet of what James had said. Juliet and Nadia immediately headed for London, dropping off Fiona with Mary while they went to see James and try to sort his mind out if it wasn't too late. They entered his room, James still suffering from the anaesthetic was fast asleep. Juliet saw the letter on the locker and opened placing her hand to her mouth on reading. She showed Nadia. Nadia remarked, shedding a tear, "I didn't know he cared so much for me."

"He's always had a big heart Nadia, that's his problem, he tries to please everyone and ends up hurting himself. I'm not letting him leave me Nadia."

"No, you mustn't. I'll find somewhere else to live, this is my fault, I have my child to look forward to."

"You won't, you'll stay with us you're part of the family in more ways than one," Juliet smiled placing her hand on Nadia's stomach. "you can stay and operate the control room I will go on missions with James. It makes perfect sense, until you've given birth and everyone should be happy."

Nadia embraced Juliet, "you are forgiving and kind, I don't think I would do the same. I would have shot you as you should have me"

The doctor popped his head around the door indicating for the two of them to come outside, which they did immediately. "I'm afraid you won't be able to have any more children with James his testicles are so badly damaged from an impact, we doubt whether he could father another child."

"Oh my God, what have I done?" Juliet went back inside with Nadia. James stirred turning over to see them both, he exhaled, "what are you doing here, there's a letter on the locker...."

"You mean this one James? before you bloody argue husband, you're coming home; you are not leaving me or your daughter, or Nadia. You created this mess and you will live with it. We intend to make your life a bloody hell James," Juliet smiled, kissing him on the forehead and so did Nadia.

James exhaled, "oh shit," he turned over and went to sleep.

What happens next is another story.

By Robert S Baker

Made in the USA
Charleston, SC
05 July 2016